W9-BJS-828

Mississippi Vivian

Mississippi Vivian

Bill Crider and
Clyde Wilson

FIVE STAR
A part of Gale, Cengage Learning

Detroit • New York • San Francisco • New Haven, Conn • Waterville, Maine • London

Five Star Publishing, a part of Gale, Cengage Learning.

Set in 11 pt. Plantin.

Printed on permanent paper.

LIBRARY OF CONGRESS CATALOGING-IN-PUBLICATION DATA

Crider, Bill, 1941–
Mississippi Vivian / Bill Crider and Clyde Wilson. — 1st ed.
p. cm.
ISBN-13: 978-1-59414-874-3 (alk. paper)
ISBN-10: 1-59414-874-0 (alk. paper)
1. Private investigators—Fiction. 2. Mississippi—Fiction. I. Wilson, Clyde, 1923– II. Title.
PS3553.R497M57 2010
813′.54—dc22 2009050632

First Edition. First Printing: April 2010.
Published in 2010 in conjunction with Tekno Books and Ed Gorman.

Printed in the United States of America
1 2 3 4 5 6 7 14 13 12 11 10

Mississippi Vivian

Chapter 1

Mississippi, August 1970

Most people hearing the name of Mississippi, that most Southern of states, will think of Southern things. The lemony scent of magnolia blossoms in the soft evening air. The taste of a mint julep in a frosted glass. An afternoon spent reading a book on a long porch shaded by thick-limbed oak trees draped with gray-green Spanish moss. Pleasant things, soothing and comforting.

Murder isn't soothing, and it doesn't offer any comfort. It's hardly ever the first thing that comes to mind when people think about the Deep South. Maybe it never comes to mind at all, not even if you're a private investigator working on a case. Not until it happens, that is.

The case I was working on didn't begin with a murder, however. That was just one of the complications.

Another complication was a piece of pie.

You might think that ordering a piece of pie in a small-town Mississippi café would be easy. I thought so, too, but it turned out that I was wrong.

The Magnolia Café was in a little town named Losgrove. The seats in the booths were covered in ancient red leatherette that had been sliced here and there with pocket knives to expose the stuffing and springs. Maybe the slicers had used the same knives that had carved initials into the hard black plastic tabletops.

Besides the carvings, every table there had a silver napkin

holder with white napkins visible on two sides. The holders were flanked by imitation cut-glass salt and pepper shakers. The smell of frying grease hung in the air. It was the kind of place where you knew the food would be good.

Nobody sat in the booths, and there was no one at any of the five or six tables, either. All six customers, including me, sat at the counter on tall barstools covered with some of the same leatherette that had been used in the booths.

There were no initials carved into the red plastic counter. Nobody would have dared to carve anything there, not while the waitress was around, anyway. She was a large middle-aged woman with prematurely white hair and a perpetual scowl. Her hair was caught up in black netting. Big glasses with tortoiseshell rims sat on the end of her nose. She wore a white apron over tight blue jeans and a white shirt.

I was drinking coffee, as were most of the other customers, all of whom were men. One of them at the end of the counter turned his head toward the waitress and asked what kind of pie she had.

"I don't know what we got," she told him. She had a big voice to match her size and a gravelly down-home Southern accent that made me think of catfish breaded, fried, and served up with a side of fried okra. "You want a piece?"

If her voice was fried catfish, his was pure grits and gravy. "How would I know if I want one 'til you tell me what you got?"

The waitress shook her head and looked at the rest of us one at a time. Nobody said anything, so she walked down to the man who'd asked about the pie.

"Tell you what," she said. "I'll get you a piece. If you don't like it, no charge."

The man shook his head and grinned. I could tell he'd been through this routine before. He even seemed to enjoy it.

"You might give me something that'd make me sick. Mincemeat, maybe. I never did like mincemeat. Sounds like something you'd feed a cat."

The woman's scowl turned into a glare. "You saying I'd give you something like that? Like cat food?"

"Not saying you would. Just saying you might, seeing as how you don't know what kind of pie you got."

"Wouldn't be any charge if you didn't like it." The waitress folded her arms. "I told you that. Now, you want it or not? Last chance."

The man thought it over, or pretended to. After a couple of seconds he said, "Well, I guess I'll take the risk, then."

The waitress reached down under the counter and brought out a pie in a covered pie plate. She took the cover off and cut a slice of the pie, set it on a plate, and pulled a fork from a glass that had several sticking out of it. She then took the pie and the fork to the man at the end of a counter. The fork clattered against the plastic when she tossed it down.

The man shook his head, picked up the fork, and had himself a bite of the pie.

"Banana cream," he said, and a couple of the men nodded.

"You satisfied?" the waitress said. "Or are you gonna ask for your money back?"

"I'm satisfied," the man said, nodding, his mouth full of pie.

The waitress nodded, as if that was the answer she'd been expecting. She walked back to the pie, covered it, and put it under the counter. Then she turned to me.

"What're you looking at?" she said.

"Nothing."

"You want a piece of pie?"

"What kind do you have?" I asked, just to see what she'd say. She didn't disappoint me.

"I don't know," she said. "You want a piece or not?"

"I guess so," I told her, looking at the black plastic name tag pinned to her shirt. "Vivian."

"My name's not Vivian," she said.

My name's not Vivian, either. It's Ted Stephens. I've been in a couple of wars in Europe and Korea, and after I'd done my duty, I wound up doing a little undercover work for the Army. Turned out I was good doing the kind of work they had for me, but I gave it up. I liked the job but not the rules and regulations, so I stopped working for the Army and become a cop in Houston, where I figured my skills would help me do the job.

They did, but the job had caused some problems with my wife, and I'd quit not long after working a big murder case. A private investigator named Clive Watson had helped me get set up with my own office because he said he was getting old and ready to retire and could throw a few clients my way. I figured I couldn't lose.

I'd been right about that. I was doing pretty well for a man my age, which is closer to fifty than I like to think about. I don't consider myself to be old, not by a long sight, but I've been shot a couple of times and I still feel a little ache in the old bullet wounds when the weather changes. That doesn't slow me down, though.

Thanks to Clive, I started doing a good business right off the bat. I have all kinds of clients, both individuals and corporations, and I handle most of the work myself. If I ever need help, there are plenty of investigators I can call on.

One of my corporate clients was the National Insurance Company. National is the reason I found myself in Losgrove, Mississippi.

National's offices weren't there, of course. You don't find big insurance companies with corporate offices in small Mississippi towns. National was headquartered back in Houston, and I'd worked for them before, doing this and that, mostly cases involving workers' comp fraud. I was friendly with Don Cogsdill, the claims manager for the company, and he's the one who called me about the job in Losgrove.

"We have some suspicious claims," he said.

Like that was big news. They had suspicious claims all the time, or at least Don thought they were suspicious. That was his job, more or less: to be suspicious of the claims. The more of them he could deny, the more money he saved the company. He was said to be good at his job. Some people might not admire that, but his bosses at National sure did.

I'd always thought it was a little strange that an insurance carrier would work so hard to avoid paying out money. After all, the people making the claims had paid their premiums for years. Don had explained it to me, though. He said that paying out money was fine and dandy if it was honest money. He was glad the company could help out people who honestly needed the payments, but he hated a cheater.

"The cheaters drive up the costs for everybody," he told me, "including the honest people. You have a policy with us, right?"

I said that I did.

"Then you should want to pay the lowest premium possible. You don't want someone cheating the company and making your premium higher than it should be."

He was right about that. But I didn't think that was all of it. I think Don just hated the idea that someone could cheat and get away with it. I didn't blame him. I didn't care for cheaters, either, and I was good at catching them. That was one reason I'd been a good cop, and it was one reason I was in the private-eye business.

Don looked like a funeral director. He had black hair that he parted on the left, and black eyes. He wore a black suit and black shoes, a white shirt, and a black tie. He was short and dapper, and I always felt like a big oaf when I was around him. I'm six-three, and nobody would ever call me dapper. I preferred jeans and open-necked shirts, and I hardly ever wore a sports jacket unless I was going to church.

We were in Don's office in a building in downtown Houston. If we hadn't been so high up, I could've seen the Harris County Courthouse and the library. As it was, all I could see was blue sky with a few flat-bottomed clouds.

Don was more agitated than usual, so I asked him how many claims there were.

"Twelve," he said. "Can you believe it? Twelve workers' comp claims, all of them from men who say they were hurt working as longshoremen down on the Ship Channel."

"That's dangerous work," I said, stringing him along. "Loading and unloading that heavy cargo. Be easy to hurt yourself doing work like that day in and day out. I'm surprised you don't have more than twelve claims."

"Hah," Don said. "That shows how much you know. They have a fine safety record down there on the Channel. We usually don't have as many as twelve claims in a whole year."

He was exaggerating there, but I let him get away with it. "I guess these must have come in pretty close together, then."

"Not so close," he said. His face was getting a little red, the way it was inclined to do when he got excited. "That's not what's bothering me. You take this one, for example."

He passed the claim form over to me, and I gave it a quick once-over. What it came down to was that a man named Percy Segal had filed a claim because he'd hurt himself while loading cotton bales.

"Percy?" I said. "That's suspicious right there."

Don didn't think I was funny. "You know I don't make fun of people's names. Keep on reading."

I kept on reading. It turned out that Percy claimed that while he was loading bales of cotton in an airplane sling, one of the bales got loose, slipped out, and fell to the dock. In the process, it hit Percy and knocked him down. He landed hard, or so he claimed, hurting his back, which made it impossible for him to work anymore.

"Uh-oh," I said when I came to that part. "Back injury."

"Right," Don said. "Back injury."

The way he said it wasn't the way I did. He said it like he was cussing, and maybe he was. Back injuries are tricky. They're easy to fake, and they're hard to disprove. Don hated back-injury claims worse than any other kind.

I put the claim form on the desk. "It could've happened just the way Percy says it did."

"You need to keep reading," Don said, sounding like a fifth-grade teacher. "There's more to it than that."

I picked up the form again.

Although Percy claimed to have been hurt so badly that he could hardly move, much less do any productive work on the docks, the doctors that the company had paid to examine him couldn't find any evidence of a serious injury. They couldn't find any evidence of any injury at all. No wonder Don was upset.

"You've been paying him compensation," I said.

Don nodded. "He has a good lawyer."

There was nothing unusual in that. Lots of people who had difficulties with their insurance companies had lawyers. Some of them even had good ones.

I returned the claim form to the desk once again. "That's just one claim."

"All the others are similar. We just paid off on them. Nobody caught the problem until just recently."

That wasn't unusual. It was a big company, and people didn't always check things out in a timely manner. They always got around to doing it, though, sooner or later.

"You said that the claims didn't come in close together, but you never did tell me what was suspicious about them."

Don leaned back in his big swivel chair and took a deep breath. His chair was much nicer than the one I had in my own office. So was his desk, but I didn't let that bother me. I'm not the kind to be envious of another man's office furnishings. Don let the breath out slowly.

"Four things," he said. He raised a finger. "Number one, all twelve men live in the same little town. Losgrove, Mississippi."

Don ignored me and held up another finger. "Number two, all twelve men with the suspicious claims have the same lawyer and doctor."

"That could happen. One guy gets a lawyer he likes and trusts, and he talks about it. People hear about what a good job the lawyer's doing, and they hire him. I get a lot of business through word of mouth, myself. And as far as having the same doctor goes, how many doctors could there be in a little Mississippi town?"

Okay, I had to admit that it still sounded a little fishy, all the claimants from the same town and having the same lawyer and doctor. On the other hand. . . . "Maybe they're related. Cousins or something. Or maybe they were all friends in high school. Their life's dream was to come to Houston and work as longshoremen on the Ship Channel after they graduated, and this lawyer is the only one they knew back home."

Don looked at me as if he thought I might have lost my mind. I'm not sure he even has a sense of humor.

"Hey," I said. "It could happen."

"You have any idea how hard it is to get in the longshoreman's union?" he said.

"Pretty hard," I said.

"You're damned right. Now where was I?"

"You just finished number two," I said.

I grinned when I said it. I couldn't help it. Don didn't. If he got the joke, which I doubted, he didn't think it was funny. He raised another finger. "Number three, those twelve men don't get mail at their home addresses. Not a single one of them. They don't even get mail at post-office boxes."

He paused as if he might be waiting for me to say something, so I obliged him.

"Okay, how do they get it, then?"

He looked a little disappointed, as if he'd expected me to come up with something better than that.

"It's not just that they all have the same lawyer," he said. "None of their checks is mailed to them. Everything, checks and all, goes through the lawyer. His name is John B. Campbell, in case you're interested."

"I'm interested," I said, and I was. "What was the name of the doctor?"

"Gillespie. Thomas Gillespie. He won't be any help. He retired and moved north to live with his daughter. He's in a nursing home now."

"Is he infirm?"

"Mentally, from what I understand. Mind's gone."

Interesting. "What was the name of that little town again?"

"Losgrove," he said. "Mississippi."

"I haven't been to Mississippi in a while," I said.

"Do you want to go back?"

"Sounds like fun," I said.

Which shows how wrong I can be sometimes.

Chapter 2

I looked at the name tag pinned to the woman's shirt, thinking that I'd made a mistake. But I hadn't. It said *Vivian,* just as I'd thought. One of the men at the counter chuckled. I couldn't tell which one it was, but I knew they were all enjoying this.

"If your name's not Vivian," I said, "what is it?"

"Who wants to know?"

"Ted Stephens. I'm happy to meet you, Vivian." I held up my hand before she could correct me again. "Or whatever your name is."

"It's Mississippi Vivian." She touched her name tag. "Not just Vivian by itself. But there wasn't room for all that."

"Mississippi's an interesting choice of names."

"That wasn't what my mama and daddy called me. The thing is, there's three women in this town named Vivian, and people had trouble keeping straight which one was being talked about. So there's a Texas Vivian, an Idaho Vivian, and me. I was born and raised right here in Losgrove, so I'm Mississippi Vivian."

Well, it made a kind of sense if you thought about it, but based on our short acquaintance, I doubted that anybody was ever going to confuse either of the other two Vivians with this one, even though I hadn't met them. Surely this one was unique.

"Then I'm pleased to meet you, Mississippi Vivian," I said. "Now how about that pie?"

"You sure you want it?"

"I said so."

She brought the pie out from under the counter again, and soon I was eating a piece of the best banana-cream pie I'd ever tasted. When I'd eaten it, including every last crumb of the flaky crust, I pushed the pie plate away. Vivian was right there to take it. When she did, I said, "Since you know about all those other Vivians, you must know just about everybody in this town."

"Maybe," she said. "Maybe not."

That was about what I'd expected. I tried a different tack.

"Ever hear of a man named Percy Segal?"

"Why do you want to know?"

I shook my head. There was no way anybody was ever going to get a direct answer from Mississippi Vivian, not even to a simple yes-or-no question.

"I need to talk to him," I said. "It's important."

"Too bad."

"Why?"

"He's not here anymore."

"Do you know where he is?"

A couple of men along the counter nudged each other and had a good chuckle at this. I figured they knew where Segal was, and they'd probably even tell me. However, I was determined to get an answer from Mississippi Vivian. I couldn't resist a challenge.

"He's a long way from here," she said. "And it's mighty hot. Not the kind of place you'd want to visit."

"I don't mind the heat," I said.

"You'd mind it where Percy is, which is likely Hell."

"He's dead?" I said.

That was something Don Cogsdill hadn't mentioned. Maybe he didn't know it himself.

"Dead as a hammer," Mississippi Vivian told me, coming up with a straight answer at last. Or maybe it wasn't an answer at all, just a confirmation.

Whatever it was, it was more than just interesting. It was quite a coincidence that the very man I'd come to town to talk to was dead. Of course there were eleven others, but Percy's name was at the top of my list, and I do run into a lot of coincidences in my line of work. Some people might be surprised at that, but coincidences happen all the time.

"What happened to him?" I said. "Heart attack?"

"I don't know," she said.

Here we go again, I thought.

"Why do you care, anyway?" she said.

"I'm just a guy who's curious about Percy Segal," I told her. I looked down the counter. The other customers were staring down into their coffee cups or gazing vacantly at their reflections in the mirror on the wall behind the counter. No more nudges or chuckles. "Maybe you and I could meet later and talk about this."

She gave me a scornful look, as if she didn't much care for what she saw. I wondered if it was the crew cut. I'd had it since my Army days, and I thought it looked pretty good.

"I don't date," she said.

I'm not easy to fluster, but for a second or two I sat there speechless. Then I managed to say, "I'm a married man." I held up my left hand so she could see the wedding band. "My wife and I have had our problems, but I don't run around."

I didn't want to talk about the problems. They were pretty much behind us now, and I wanted to keep them there.

Mississippi Vivian almost smiled. "I guess you have enough to keep up with at home."

"You got that right. All I want to do is buy a few minutes of your time and talk. Just talk. That's all there is to it."

"I'm not going off somewhere with you, if that's what you're hoping."

"I told you that I don't run around, and that includes going off with women for talks. We can talk right here and right now."

The suggestion didn't please her. She wiped the counter in front of me with a rag for a few seconds, looking at the other customers, none of whom looked back. Either she had them all cowed or she didn't want to talk about Segal in front of them.

"I get to take a break in an hour," she said, pointing to a Dr Pepper clock on the wall to my left. "All the coffee drinkers will most likely be gone by then, and we can talk in the back booth. That one under the clock."

I told her I'd be there, dropped a five on the counter, and left.

Stepping out of the air-conditioned café into the summer humidity wasn't much different from doing the same thing in Houston, which is to say it was like suddenly inhaling warm, wet cotton. I stood still for a minute to get used to it, not that anybody ever really got used to something like that. In some ways, though, it felt good to me. Long ago, in a faraway war, I'd been shot in the right leg. Sometimes even now, the wound acted up a little bit, but that hardly ever happened when it was warm and humid.

My car was parked in front of the café, and it had an air conditioner, but I didn't get into the car. I didn't have far to go. A tough private eye like me could stand a little heat and humidity, and besides, John B. Campbell's office was only a block from the café. I'd spotted it when I drove into town, and in fact it was the reason I'd gone to the café in the first place.

In a small town like Losgrove, everybody knows what's going on, and a café is a prime place for gossip. I'd planned to ask about Percy Segal and John B. Campbell and see what I could find out. Mississippi Vivian wasn't going to talk, though, not in front of anybody else, and the customers were a close-mouthed bunch. Nobody except Mississippi Vivian had said a word to me the whole time I'd been in the café.

My visit hadn't been a total waste of time, however. While I hadn't learned anything about Campbell, I'd found out that Percy Segal was dead. I wasn't sure how that information was going to be of any use to me, though. Not until I found out how he'd died. I was hoping that maybe Mississippi Vivian could tell me that.

And maybe she could, but would she? That was the important question. Getting an answer from her was harder than cracking walnuts with a pillow.

Campbell's office was in a squat building made of red brick. It was next door to a barbershop, one with a red-and-white pole out front. It had been a while since I'd seen one of those poles. Barbershops had started disappearing in Houston a few years ago, back when long hair for men became fashionable. Not for me, of course, but for plenty of others.

Campbell's name was painted in gold letters on the plate-glass window that faced the street, with "Attorney at Law" underneath. The paint was cracked and chipped, a lot like the building itself. Obviously Campbell didn't believe in putting up much of a front.

I opened the door and went inside. I found myself in a large room that was almost empty. I closed the door behind me and looked around, but there was nothing much to see. There was a desk with a telephone sitting on it. There was a little radio, too, but no receptionist and no chairs for clients to sit in while they waited. An electric typewriter sat on the desk, but I didn't see any typing paper. And that was it. Campbell didn't go in for anything fancy. He was a small-town lawyer, and he didn't pretend to be anything else.

There were a couple of pictures on the walls, but they weren't anything to brag about, nothing more than amateurish prints of plantation houses with oaks and magnolia trees, just in case anybody who dropped by wondered what state they were in. The pictures looked as if they might belong on the walls of a local motel.

The beige carpet under my feet was clean enough, but it was old and worn. The room was cool, though, and I was grateful for that. The sweat under my shirt dried almost instantly. I could hear the air conditioner humming somewhere, so I knew that at least Campbell paid his electric bill.

A little to the left on the back wall of the big room were two doors. One of them was open, and I figured it must lead to Campbell's office. As I stood there looking around, a loud voice boomed out from the office, "Come on in!"

I walked over to the door and looked inside. If I'd been expecting someone big enough to match the voice, I would've been disappointed. A man got out of his chair behind a desk made of some kind of dark wood and stood up. He was no more than five and a half feet tall, a full eight inches shorter than I am. His height might have been a disadvantage for him in a jury trial, but his voice probably made up for it.

He wore leather shoes with a little bit of a heel, but they didn't add much to his height. I guessed his weight at around a hundred and forty pounds, some of which was centered in a little paunch that hung over his belt. He had on a pair of khakis and a white shirt, but no tie. A navy sports jacket hung over the back of his swivel chair. His brownish hair was going gray all over, but he didn't look more than forty.

He gave me a wide smile. Maybe he thought I was a prospective client. He stuck out his hand for me to shake and said, "I'm John B. Campbell," he said. "What can I do for you?"

I took his hand. It was the size of a child's.

"I'm Ted Stephens," I told him, trying not to crush his hand. "I'm a private investigator from Houston."

He pulled his hand away. If he was disappointed, he didn't

show it. He didn't seem impressed, either.

I took one of my cards from my billfold and handed it to him. He looked at the card, nodded, and stuck it his shirt pocket.

"Have a seat, Mr. Stephens," he said, indicating a couple of worn wingback chairs covered in cracked maroon leather.

I sat down, and he went back behind his desk. His chair seat must have been jacked up as high as it would go so he could see over the top of the desk. I would have bet that his feet weren't touching the floor. The wall behind him was lined with shelves of dusty law books. The room's only window was on the wall to my right. A fly buzzed against it, trying to get outside. He wasn't having a whole lot of success. Sitting against the wall opposite the window were a couple of wooden filing cabinets with an oak finish that didn't match the desk.

"What's a private investigator from the big city of Houston doing here in our little town?" he said when I was seated. He was still smiling as if he was glad to see me, even though I wasn't a client, and he seemed to want to help me if he could.

I'd already told Campbell my name and given him my card. There might be some investigators who like to play things close to the vest, use false names, and beat around the bush, but I'm not one of them. I believe in the straightforward approach, at least now and then, and I wanted to be up-front with Campbell about why I was there.

"I represent the National Insurance Company," I said. "A lot of people from your little town have filed claims with National. Every one of them's a longshoreman, and they all claim to have been injured on the job. I believe you represent some of them."

Campbell leaned forward on the desk. He was one of those clean-desk men. The only thing on it besides a telephone was an ashtray, and it was empty. The black top of the desk was lacquered, and so shiny that I could see his reflection in it.

"I represent a lot of people," he said. He wasn't smiling

anymore, and I was pretty sure he wasn't glad to see me. Maybe he never had been, not really. "Some of them happen to be longshoremen. As a matter of fact, I think I have five or six clients who might have filed claims with your firm."

It wasn't my firm, but I didn't bother to correct him about that. I was going to correct him about the number of his clients who'd filed claims, though. He'd understated the number by about half.

"Mr. Campbell," I said, but that was as far as I got before he held up a hand. I stopped and waited to hear why he was interrupting me.

"You don't have to call me Mr. Campbell," he said. "Everybody around here calls me John B. I wish you would, too. Puts things on a friendlier footing."

So we were back to being friendly again. I didn't really care about being his friend, but if that was what he wanted, I'd go along. For the moment, anyway.

"Call me Ted, John B.," I said.

"Sure, Ted. Now go on with your story."

It wasn't a story, but I didn't call him on that one, either.

"I have a list of twelve claimants," I told him. "Not five or six. And you represent every one of them. The first one to file a claim was a man named Percy Segal."

John B. nodded. "Fine fella. I used to represent him, all right. Had to work pretty hard to get him his money. Our doctor didn't agree with National's doctors."

No surprise there. "About that doctor," I said.

"Doctor Gillespie. Fine man, but a sad story. Senile."

"What about when he did the exams?"

"He was just fine then. Anybody will tell you that."

They might, but I wouldn't believe them. I figured the doctor had been at a stage where he'd agree to treat just about any complaint you had and take your word for it. No wonder the claims had all come from the same man.

"I don't represent Segal anymore, though," John B. continued. "He's dead." He paused and looked down, as if out of respect for the dear departed. "He died a few weeks ago. I do represent his estate, though."

I wasn't interested in the estate, not at this point, anyway.

"John B.," I said, "National has some canceled checks made out to Percy Segal. He'd endorsed them, but they were all mailed to you right here at this office. The good folks at National Insurance were kind of wondering about that."

John B. looked up at me. If we'd ever been friends, it was all over between us now. Not that I cared.

"I don't know what the hell you're implying, Ted," he said. Even if we weren't pals, we were still on a first-name basis. "Or rather, I *do* know what you're implying, and I don't like it a damn' bit. There haven't been any checks sent here from National Insurance."

"I wasn't implying anything. Just stating a fact."

"It's not a fact. It's a damn' lie. You'd better stop making false accusations, or I'll file a lawsuit against your company so fast it'll make your head swim."

He was doing it again, calling National *my* company. I still didn't feel like correcting him about that, but I couldn't let all of what he said go by without a challenge.

"I don't remember making any accusations," I said.

"Well, you did. You can't go around saying things like that without proof. Let me see those canceled checks."

"I don't have them with me."

That was only sort of true. I had them, all right, but they were in my briefcase, and it was locked in the trunk of my car.

"Sure you don't." He gave me a smug grin. "That's the same as saying they don't exist. You could get in big trouble, Ted, saying things you can't back up with proof."

For the time being I let John B. think he'd gotten the better of me.

"I'm sorry," I said. "I should have known that I'd need solid proof, what with you being an attorney and all. Let's just forget I mentioned it."

John B. shook his head. "It's hard to forget something like that. I don't like being accused of being a crook."

"Careful now. I wasn't accusing you of anything. I just mentioned something the company thought was unusual. Let's change the subject."

He didn't look happy, but he didn't object, so I said, "There's something that's been bothering me ever since I was assigned to this case. How in the hell did men from here wind up working as longshoremen at the Houston Ship Channel?"

John B. relaxed a little. "How much do you know about Mississippi?" he asked.

"Not a whole lot," I said.

"You been in town long?"

"Just got here this morning."

"You drive around any, look things over?"

I had, and I knew what he was getting at. I decided I'd let him tell me, though, so I just nodded and said, "I saw a little of the town."

"You saw what the place is like, then. Not exactly a thriving metropolis, is it? No industry, the farming's not what it used to be, and there's not much of anything going on. We have a lumberyard, a couple of convenience stores, some insurance offices, a drugstore." He jerked a thumb at the wall. "A barbershop. You get what I'm saying?"

I told him I got it, but he had some more to say on the subject.

"There's not much work here for anybody, not the kind of work a man can make a living at, anyway. You can pick up a few dollars now and then, but there's not much that's steady. It's that way pretty much all over Mississippi. The damn' hurricanes haven't helped us any, either."

"I can understand that," I said, thinking of Hurricane Celia, which had ripped into Texas only a couple of weeks earlier. Four or five people had died in Corpus Christi and Port O'Connor. Camille had hit Mississippi last year, and it had been even worse. A lot worse.

I thought of the men in the café, not young but not old, either, heavy-bodied, able men, but instead of working they were hanging around, drinking coffee, killing time. Maybe drawing some kind of benefits to keep themselves and their families going until they could find some kind of job, or waiting till they could fill in for the dishwasher at the Magnolia Café.

"Believe me," I told John B., "I sympathize. I like small towns, but they're dying out all over the country. It's not just Mississippi. It's a real problem, all right, but it doesn't answer my question about how Percy got his job on the Ship Channel. It's not easy to get on with the longshoreman's union even if you're born and raised in Houston. It's a lot harder if you're from out of town, much less from out of the state."

"Percy had connections," John B. said.

That sounded vaguely sinister to me, so I asked what he meant.

"It doesn't have anything to do with organized crime, if that's what you're thinking. Percy's cousin works there. Went to Houston when he was just a kid and went to school there. He was a pretty good high-school football player, but not good enough for college."

"Good enough to have friends on the docks, though," I said.

"That's right. So they got him a job when he graduated, and he stuck with it. He's a big shot in the union now. Percy's brother works on the docks, too. He doesn't have much stroke, but between the two of them, him and the cousin, they got

Percy into the union and got him a job."

"What about all the others?"

"Percy arranged it, with the help of his cousin and his brother. With three of them working there, it was easier. Everybody who went over there was one of Percy's buddies from around here. The way I understand it. . . ."

His voice trailed off. I waited a while, glancing out the window. There was nothing to see except an empty street.

"Go on," I said, looking back at John B., after the pause lengthened. "Don't stop now. It was just starting to get interesting."

"There was some deal Percy had with his friends. I don't know all the details, and I don't know that I should talk about it."

"It might help if I knew."

He thought about it for a few seconds. "Well, I guess it won't hurt anything. There was nothing illegal about it. Supposedly Percy had some kind of a deal with his buddies. They were paying him a percentage of their earnings. Sort of a reward for him getting them the jobs. I don't know how long that was supposed to go on, but as far as I know, they didn't have any objections. They were just glad to get the work."

I didn't see how that tied in with anything I was working on, but maybe it would be important later. Then it dawned on me that maybe Percy was paying somebody off, maybe some of the union officials. If that was the case, we'd have a real scandal on our hands. I'd have to keep that in mind.

Then I thought about the desk in the other room and said, "Do you have a secretary?"

"I sure do, and she's a good one."

"Hard to find a good one in Losgrove?"

"Nope. Plenty of women would like to have a job here, so I was able to pick and choose. Carolyn was the best of the bunch that applied."

"Carolyn?" I said.

"Her name's Carolyn Lacy," John B. said. "My secretary. She's not coming in today. Said she wasn't feeling well."

I wanted to have a little chat with Carolyn Lacy, but I wouldn't bother her while she was on her sickbed. Besides, it was about time for me to get back to the Magnolia Café and see if Mississippi Vivian was going to keep her appointment with me. I told John B. that I had to leave but that I'd be back to see him soon.

The last bit of news didn't seem to make him especially happy. "I hope I've made it clear to you that I don't know anything about those checks you claim came through this office."

"I'm taking your word for it," I said.

"My word's good. You can ask anybody in Losgrove."

I nodded and stood up to leave. John B. didn't get up or offer to shake hands again. I figured he didn't want to have to jump down out of his chair. He just sat there, so I told him good-bye and left. I could sense his eyes watching my back when I went out the door.

Chapter 3

As I walked back down the block to the Magnolia Café, I saw only a couple of cars parked along the curb, and one of them was my rental. No one drove along the dusty street. I breathed in the humidity without the scent of exhaust fumes.

When I entered the café, I could see at a glance that Mississippi Vivian had been right. The place was deserted except for her. She sat in the booth she'd mentioned, the one in the back. I walked back and joined her, sliding onto the cracked leatherette seat. A mug of coffee sat in front of Mississippi Vivian. She didn't offer to get one for me.

"Well, Mr. Investigator," she said, looking at me over the rim of her glasses, "where you been? Down the street talking to John B.?"

"Call me Ted," I said. "Are there any secrets in this town, or does everybody already know why I'm here and where I am at all times?"

It would've been easy enough for her to have seen from the front window that I'd been to the lawyer's office. But I wondered who'd been talking about my job. John B. was supposedly the only one who knew who I was, except for the desk clerk at the motel where I was staying. I hadn't seen any reason for secrecy, so I'd used my real name and the name of the company I was representing. I'd even given the desk clerk a business card in case he ever needed an ace private investigator.

I'd checked in early the previous evening, but I hadn't gone out, so it was likely the desk clerk who'd spread the word. He looked like the type to drop by the café after he got off work and talk about the newcomers he'd seen that day.

Mississippi Vivian took a sip of coffee and set the mug back on the table. She gave me what for her amounted to a straight answer.

"If there are any secrets in Losgrove, Ted, I don't know 'em."

"They wouldn't be secrets if you did," I pointed out.

"Well, that's right. But what I mean is, it's hard to keep a secret here. Everybody in town likes to talk. There's not a whole lot else to do. When a stranger comes to town, we all know who he is and what his business is by the time he gets past the city limit sign."

"Then I guess you know what I'm here to talk to you about."

"Nope. That's something that hasn't gotten around yet. Give it another hour or two, though, and you can bet it will."

She meant that John B. would spread the word. I didn't have another hour or two to waste, however, so I told her that I was a private investigator working for National Insurance. I added a little about the cases I was looking into for the company.

"Now," I said when I was finished, "I want to tell you something else. I'm here on an expense account, and the company's authorized me to pay for information. You should look at this little chat we're having as strictly a business transaction. You have something valuable to sell, and I'm going to pay you for it."

"What do I have that's valuable?"

"Information," I said.

"Information? That's all?"

I nodded.

"I'm not sure I have any information that would interest you."

"You can let me be the judge of that. I'll pay you, no matter what."

The last part got her attention. "Let's say I have some of this information that you're willing to pay for. Or even if I don't . . . how much will I be getting for talking to you?"

"A hundred dollars."

"In advance?"

I leaned forward in the booth and pulled my wallet from my back pocket. I got out a hundred-dollar bill and passed it across the table to her. She looked it over as if she hadn't seen one before, or at least not for a long time. She probably hadn't. I suspected that people in Losgrove weren't big tippers. After she was through looking, she folded it neatly in half, then in half again.

"And I get to keep it even if I don't know anything worthwhile?" she said, holding the folded bill between her thumb and forefinger.

"You still keep the money."

"That seems fair enough." She stuck the bill into the big pocket on the front of her apron. "Go ahead and start the ball rolling."

I thought about some of the many questions I had, including a few that I hadn't asked John B. I figured I might as well begin with the big one, the one I'd had a feeling John B. wouldn't want to answer. That wasn't the reason I hadn't asked him, however. I just hadn't wanted to make him too suspicious.

"How did Percy Segal die?" I said.

"Perce," she said, pronouncing it like *purse*. "That's what we called him. He didn't like *Percy*. Thought it sounded too sissy."

We were back to the old roundabout way of getting to the point. But she'd still told me something I hadn't known. John B. hadn't told me about Percy's preference. Maybe John B. just tended to be more formal when he was talking about his clients.

"Perce sounds like a woman's purse," I said. "Didn't Percy think that was sissy?"

"What do you think?"

"I guess not," I said. "Perce, then. How did he die?"

"Rifle bullet in the chest. Suicide so they say, except they fancied it all up. 'Self-inflicted gunshot wound' is what they called it."

"Who's *they?*"

"The sheriff and everybody else in town. Joe Bronte's the sheriff." She spelled the last name for me. "He pronounces it *bront* instead of the way those writing sisters pronounced it. You know. *Wuthering Heights.*"

I didn't know, but I didn't say so. I didn't want her to think I didn't read the classics, but the truth is my taste runs more to vulgar New York writers like Mickey Spillane than to refined English women.

"Joe worked the whole investigation himself, personally," she continued. "I don't know much about that part. Just what the outcome was and what the gossip was. I hear a lot of that here at the café."

I'd already guessed that, so I asked if there'd been any other gossip.

"I think I'll get me another cup of coffee," she said. "You want one? On the house. You don't have to worry about that expense account."

I told her I'd take a cup, and she got up to get it. I hoped she'd give me some answers when she came back, but with her you couldn't be sure.

"You want anything in yours?" she asked, holding up her cup. "You've only been here once before, or I'd remember."

"Black is fine," I said.

I could never get used to sweet coffee. Strong and bitter was fine with me.

Mississippi Vivian took her mug and went to a coffeemaker that sat on a shelf behind the counter. A glass carafe sat on the warmer. She poured a mug for herself, then got one for me. She brought both mugs back to the booth and set one in front of me before sliding into the seat across from me.

"Now," she said after taking a sip of the coffee, "where were we?"

I had a drink from the mug. The coffee was bitter, all right, the same way it had been that morning. It was also lukewarm, which was just the way I liked it. The inside of my mouth burns easily.

"You were about to tell me the gossip about Perce Segal's death."

"It's not so much gossip as it is what people heard and repeated."

I wasn't sure I got the distinction. "Whatever it is," I said, trying to be patient, "I'd like to hear about it."

"Well, according to what I heard, Perce killed himself at Wade Dickie's house."

That was an interesting piece of information right there, I thought, and it wasn't just that Perce had killed himself at another man's house. That was odd enough to get my attention all by itself, for sure, but what made it even more unusual was that Wade Dickie's name was on my list of claimants.

"What was Mr. Dickie doing when Perce shot himself?" I said.

"Oh, he wasn't home. He'd gotten a job unloading a truck at the lumberyard that day. Perce was supposed to help him, but he didn't show up."

"Too busy shooting himself, I guess."

Mississippi Vivian didn't crack a smile. Nobody ever gets my jokes. It didn't bother me. What bothered me was that two of my claimants, both of whom were supposed to have sustained disabling injuries while working on the docks, had signed on to unload a lumber truck. That wasn't exactly the kind of work a man with a bad back should have been doing.

"Does Wade Dickie have any family?" I said.

Mississippi Vivian nodded. "A wife and a daughter."

"Where were they when Perce was shooting himself?"

"The wife's name is Ann. She's a clerk at the drugstore. Been there for years. Ever since it was Coggin and Smith Drugs. It's still called that, but Mr. Smith died five years ago."

I wondered if that was an answer, so I said, "She was at the drugstore?"

"I just told you that."

She hadn't, but I didn't figure it was worth arguing about. I didn't think very many people had ever won an argument with her.

"What about the daughter?" I asked.

"Barbara. I don't know where she was. She's eighteen years old and doesn't live at home all the time these days. She left town after Perce killed himself. I guess the thought of living here after something like that was too much for her. She's back now, though. She's a beautiful girl, but kind of wild. Or so they say. I wouldn't know about that, myself."

I suspected that she knew more about the daughter's alleged wildness than she was telling, but I didn't want to get into that. Yet.

"You wouldn't think someone who was wild would let a little thing like a suicide bother her so much."

"You never know about folks," Vivian said. "I've heard that a lot of artists are wild, but they're pretty sensitive. Have to be, if they're artists."

I didn't want to get into any philosophical discussions, either. I was more interested in some concrete facts.

"Why did Perce kill himself?" I said. "Anybody have the

answer to that?"

"Well, maybe he didn't," she said. "Kill himself, that is. All we have is the sheriff's word on that. He wasn't depressed or anything, not as far as anybody knew. He seemed to be getting along just fine. He had his troubles, though."

"What kind of troubles?"

"Depends on what you mean by *troubles.*"

I didn't remind her that she was the one who'd used the word. I said, "Any kind."

"He drank some. Didn't use to, but his wife left him a while back, and he got to drinking a little too much."

"Why did his wife leave him?"

"Don't know. Anything I told you would be just gossip."

"That's exactly what I want to hear."

"Well, the word around town was that Percy was fooling around a little, if you know what I mean."

I knew what she meant, all right. "Who was he fooling with?" I said.

"I wouldn't know that. Nobody ever said. I heard that things got worse after his wife died, though. The drinking, I mean."

"What about the fooling around?"

"Could be that got worse, too. Those things go together, kind of. Maybe that was it. He got depressed about his wife and the way he was living his life and decided to end it all."

"End it all?" I said.

"That's what they call it when people kill themselves," Vivian said. "I read it in a book once."

It must have been a pretty old book, I thought.

"Did anybody think it was funny that he killed himself in somebody else's house?" I said.

"You mean funny ha-ha or funny strange?"

"My jokes can be pretty bad," I said, "but I'm not joking about this."

"People did talk about that," she said. "Nobody had much of an idea why he might do it that way, unless he just didn't want to mess up his own house."

I looked to see if she was making a joke. She wasn't.

"It was awful, from what I heard," she continued. "Took a good while to get the place cleaned up. Anyway, Perce must have been out of his mind to do what he did. You don't kill yourself if you're not crazy. So maybe he had some other crazy reason for doing it at Wade's place."

I thought that not wanting to mess up your own house was crazy enough. I could see that I was going to have to talk to the sheriff later and check out his version of things, but right now I needed a little more information about the claimants. I took the list of their names out of my pocket and looked it over.

"What about a man named Tommy Holmes?" I said. "Ever hear of him?"

"Tommy? Sure. He works at the lumberyard, too. Been working there ever since he was a kid, except for that time he went off and worked in Houston for a while. He didn't stay very long."

Just long enough to hurt his back, I thought, wondering if everybody in town worked at the lumberyard. That was a place I might need to look into. I looked at the next name on my list.

"Ed Holt," I said. "Don't tell me he works at the lumberyard, too."

This time Mississippi Vivian smiled. "Nope. He works for Kathy Hull, down at the tractor company."

"Who's Kathy?"

"I thought you'd have found that out by now."

I sighed. Things had been going so well, and now the runaround had started again.

"She's not on my list," I said, giving my piece of paper a little shake. "I never heard of her."

"You aren't much of an investigator, then, are you."

"I guess not. Why don't you just tell me who she is and save us some time."

"She's Carolyn Lacy's daughter. Carolyn works for John B."

She looked at me over the tops of her glasses.

"I know that," I said.

"Well, I'm glad you found out something. Anyway, Kathy works for John B., too. Fridays usually. Her mother takes that day off, and Kathy takes over at John B.'s office."

"Carolyn's not there today."

Mississippi Vivian knew all about it. "Nope. She's home sick. Got that twenty-four-hour bug that's been going around. Lots of people have been getting it. One man even claimed it was something he ate here at the café that gave it to him, but everybody knew better than that."

"Why isn't Kathy filling in for her mother today?"

Mississippi Vivian looked at me as if I didn't have a whole lot of sense.

"She can't get off from the tractor company except on Fridays, that's why."

"Right. I should have figured that out for myself."

"You sure should. You want a refill on that coffee?"

"No, thanks. Tell me about Kathy Hull and Carolyn Lacy."

She didn't say anything for a few seconds. Maybe she was organizing her thoughts, or maybe she was trying to decide how much she wanted to tell me.

"First off," she said, "they're both real good Christians, even if Kathy is divorced." She paused as if to give me time to contradict her. When I didn't, she went on. "They both go to the First Baptist Church."

I could have told her that while as far as I knew being divorced didn't have a thing to do with being a good Christian, being a Baptist didn't make being a Christian a sure thing. I'd worked a case not long ago in which the bad guys turned out to be a couple of Baptist deacons who'd been working a home-repair scam.

"I go to First Baptist, myself," Mississippi Vivian said, so I thought it best not to mention the deacons.

"Carolyn works for John B., but then you know that already."

I nodded.

"Kathy, she's smart as a whip. She's the business manager at the tractor company. Runs the whole thing, good as any man could. Better, maybe. Makes good money, too. They let her off on Fridays so she can fill in for her mama."

"Why doesn't her mother work on Fridays?"

"She likes a long weekend. Needs time to get her housework done, that kind of thing. She cleans up at the church some, too."

Mississippi Vivian sighed, as if to let me know that she could use a long weekend now and again. She put her fingers into the pocket of the apron to touch the hundred-dollar bill. Maybe she'd get a chance to take some time off now that she had a little money set aside.

"Is there anybody else who works in John B.'s office?" I said.

Mississippi Vivian shook her head. "He doesn't have a big practice. Those women are all the help he needs. Probably all he can afford."

A couple of men pushed through the door of the café. They looked toward Vivian, then found themselves a table and sat down.

"Lunch crowd's here," she said. She stood up. "I hope you got your hundred dollars' worth."

"I might have a few more questions later."

"All right. You staying for lunch?"

"What's today's special?"

"What do you like?"

"Can't you just tell me what the special is? It would make things a lot easier."

Mississippi Vivian looked a little put out that I'd challenge her like that, but she forced herself to give me an answer.

"Meatloaf and mashed potatoes, just like your mama used to make."

"I hope not," I said. "Mama wasn't much of a cook."

"How about your grandmama?"

"She fixed a mean meatloaf."

"Then this one's better than hers. You want to try it or not?"

"Might as well," I said.

Chapter 4

The meatloaf was as good as promised, and the mashed potatoes were fine, too. Mississippi Vivian hadn't even mentioned the yeasty rolls, which were even better. Even my grandmama couldn't have done as well, not that I'd ever have told her that, rest her soul. The green beans were a little mushy, but I didn't see any need to complain. I had a glass of iced tea to go along with it all and felt as if my trip to Mississippi had paid off even if I didn't solve the case.

Thinking of the case depressed me a little and took the edge off my feeling of well-fed contentment. I hadn't bargained on having one of the claimants turn up dead the way Perce Segal had, much less under such suspicious circumstances. I had a feeling that things weren't going to be as easy to resolve as I'd thought they might be. Dead people have a way of complicating things.

I left a hefty tip on the table (expense account, remember?) and paid my check. Mississippi Vivian worked the cash register in addition to serving the tables. It wasn't too hard on her because the place wasn't crowded. She asked if I'd liked the food.

"What do you think?"

She gave me a hard look as if she wondered if I might be messing with her, which I was, of course.

"I think you liked it," she said. "Did you?"

I told her that it was excellent and that I'd be back. She nodded as if that was what she'd been expecting to hear.

"Got a hard afternoon of investigating ahead of you?" she said.

"You guessed it."

"Where you going next?"

I told her she'd have to guess that, too. It was a joke, but she didn't laugh. I wondered if I worked on my delivery, people would catch on. Probably not, I decided.

As I left the café, I noticed that a car was parked in front of John B.'s office. I figured it wouldn't hurt to see who was consulting him. If the claimants knew I was in town, as most people seemed to, it might be one of them, checking with his lawyer to see if he knew why some private eye from Houston was snooping around in Losgrove.

It wasn't a claimant's car, however. When I reached the office, I saw through the window that a woman sat behind the desk in the big anteroom. It just about had to be either Carolyn Lacy or her daughter, Kathy Hull.

I thought for a while about what I might do, humming a little bit of "Blue Hawaii," then went to my car and got the briefcase from the trunk. It was a thin leather case with no handles and the National Insurance Logo on one side. I tucked it under my left arm before closing the trunk lid. The hot metal stung my fingers when I touched it, but I was too tough to show it. I walked back to John B.'s office.

The woman behind the desk looked up and smiled when I walked in. I guessed her age at about fifty-five, but I'm terrible about guessing women's ages. Their makeup and the way they dress can throw me off easily. She had reddish hair, as did a lot of women who'd been brunettes earlier in life, and blue eyes that crinkled at the corners with her smile. She looked a little peaked, as if she might have been under the weather lately.

"Come in," she said. "What can we do for you today?"

She had a soft Mississippi accent like Vivian's, and she didn't seem to have a clue as to who I was.

"Are you Carolyn Lacy?" I said.

She said that she was, and I told her my name. I explained that I'd been in earlier to talk to John B. and that I'd hoped to talk to her, too, but I'd been told that she wasn't feeling well.

"It was just a little stomach virus. I got over it real quick. What did you want to talk to me about?"

She didn't say *little ole me,* but with that accent she might as well have.

"It's about some checks from some of John B.'s clients," I said. "Do you think he could spare me a few minutes?"

"Why, I'm sure he can, but let me ask him before I send you in."

John B. didn't have a fancy intercom system. Carolyn got up and walked over to his office, the door to which was now closed. She tapped on it with one knuckle and went in without waiting for an answer. She closed the door behind her. I stood and hummed a few bars of "Sugar, Sugar" while I waited. Everybody tells me I have terrible taste in music, but I don't let it bother me. If I was under thirty, maybe I'd hum something by Bob Dylan.

Carolyn opened John B.'s door after a minute or so and said, "Come on in, Mr. Stephens."

I joined them in the office. Carolyn stood beside John B.'s desk. He didn't look exactly thrilled to see me again.

"What can I do for you, Ted?" he said, without getting up.

I was glad to see that we were still on a first-name basis, even if he didn't seem happy that I was there. Since we were such good friends, I sat in one of the wingback chairs without waiting to be invited. I put the briefcase in my lap and patted it with my left hand.

"I have some of those canceled checks here," I said. "The ones we were talking about earlier."

John B. frowned. "I thought you told me you didn't have them."

"I said I didn't have them with me. That was then. This is now. And now I do have them with me."

John B. looked at me as if he thought I was unduly sneaky, if not in fact an outright liar, but I was reasonably confident that he'd made his share of true but misleading remarks during the course of his legal career. Probably as often as I had, if not more often. I opened the briefcase and brought out one of the canceled checks made out to Percy Segal. I leaned forward and slid the check across the top of the desk, which was so slick that the check glided as if on ice.

John B. put a finger on the check to stop it from sliding right over the edge of the desk. Then he picked it up and looked it over. Carolyn, who was standing beside him, took a good look as well.

"I have to admit," John B. said after he'd completed his examination of the check, "that I didn't really believe you had one of these. I guess I was wrong."

I shrugged, as if to say that anybody could be wrong now and then.

"I never even knew Percy got any money from your company, and that's the truth. He never told me what a good job I did for him. He never told me he was getting any checks."

I didn't have anything to say to that, so I just sat there. John B. looked at the check again. He looked at the front, then flipped it over to look at the back. Flip. Flip. Flip. I thought he was going to wear it out, but he finally stopped and set the check back on his desk.

"You say this check was mailed right here to this office?" he said.

"That's right," I told him. "And it's not the only one." I looked at Carolyn, who was looking down at the check as if fascinated by it. "All the other claimants' checks were mailed here, too. There were quite a few of them."

John B. picked up the check again. This time he was particularly interested in the endorsement on the back. It was written in black ball-point ink, and he ran his finger over it, as if that might tell him whether the signature was genuine.

"Carolyn," he said without looking at her, "did you ever get any mail here that was addressed to Percy Segal?"

"No, sir," she said, shaking her head. "Never. Not any mail addressed to him in care of the office or any mail to him directed at this address." She looked at me and grinned. I grinned back, just to be sociable. "I open all the mail that comes into the office, you know. I'm kind of the screener, I guess you'd call me. I make sure John B. doesn't have to deal with the junk mail and solicitations and all like that."

"Are you here every day?" I said, although I knew the answer already.

"No, not every day. I take off one day a week to volunteer at the church. First Baptist. Two other women and I clean up the place and help out however we can. John B. thinks it's a good idea for me to take an interest in the church and community, don't you, John B.?"

John B. nodded, but I could tell that he wasn't thinking much about what she said. He was still looking at the check, as if he couldn't quite figure out where it had come from. Or maybe it was the signature that bothered him.

"What day do you take off?" I asked Carolyn. I knew the answer to that one, too, thanks to Mississippi Vivian, but I never like to let people know everything I've found out about them.

"Friday," Carolyn told me. "That way the church is still clean and straight on Sunday."

"So does that mean John B. opens the mail on Friday?"

"Oh," Carolyn said.

She opened her mouth to say something else, but she didn't. Neither did I. It's usually best just to wait in that situation. Sooner or later someone will say something.

"Kathy opens the mail on Friday," John B. said before the silence stretched out for too long. "Kathy Hull. She's Carolyn's daughter. She works full-time down at the Parsons Tractor Company and part-time here. I trust her the same as I do Carolyn, and they both have the authority to open the mail for me."

"How does the tractor company manage to get along without her?" I said. "If she's full-time there, I mean."

Carolyn smiled. "She doesn't come in until after lunch. John B. doesn't really need anybody on Friday mornings. It's always slow around here then. So Kathy comes in for half a day and takes care of the mail and whatever else needs to be done. It's slow at the tractor company on Fridays, just like it is here, especially in the afternoon."

"So the mail comes in the afternoon?"

"Sometimes. Sometimes it's earlier. If it comes in the morning on Fridays, the mailman just leaves it on the desk, and Kathy takes care of it."

I thought that over, then said to John B., "So you don't ever open your own mail?"

"Nope. I don't like to bother with it."

"Seems to me that could be dangerous. There might be something in there that you didn't want anybody to see."

By *anybody,* I meant Carolyn of course, and Kathy.

John B. laughed, a good booming sound, surprising from such a small man. "I guess you Houston folks don't know much about life in a small town. People here know pretty much all there is to know about me, and about everybody else in Losgrove. You ever hear that expression that goes, 'My life is an open book?' "

"Sure," I said.

"Well, that's just the way it is here in Losgrove. If I don't change my underwear every day—excuse me, Carolyn, for my crudity—if I don't change my underwear every day, then everybody in town will know that I'm not a man of cleanly habits. Nothing in the mail about me would be a surprise to Carolyn or Kathy."

I wondered if they knew about his underwear, or if one of them did, but this wasn't the time to ask that question.

"What about your clients?" I said. "Don't they want confidentiality?"

"They have it. If they wrote something to me that the town didn't already know, which is doubtful, then they know that Carolyn and Kathy are just as tight-lipped as I am about whatever it is they say. Isn't that right, Carolyn?"

"It sure is, John B. I wouldn't have lasted here as long as I have if I didn't know how to keep a secret."

"I heard there weren't any secrets in Losgrove," I told her. "And John B. implied the same thing."

"Maybe there aren't," John B. said. "We were just giving you a hypothetical."

That wasn't all they were giving me. One of them just about had to be lying. Unfortunately, I wasn't sure which one it was.

On the other hand, maybe both of them were telling the truth. Maybe Kathy Hull was the one I should have been talking to about the checks, though it was hard to see how anybody could have timed it so that all the checks arrived on Friday.

Of course it was also possible that they were both lying and that both were in on the scheme together, along with Kathy. Nobody had ever promised me that my job would be easy.

Who was lying? I'd just have to figure it out later on. At the moment there was something else I wanted to ask about, the thing that I thought might have been worrying John B. about the check. I asked him about the endorsement.

"Can you verify that the signature on that check is Percy Segal's?" I said.

John B. looked at the back of the check one more time. He nodded and said, "Maybe. Carolyn, pull Percy's file for us."

Carolyn walked over to the wooden filing cabinets and pulled open the bottom drawer of the one on her right. She slipped an olive-colored file folder out, brought it over to John B.'s desk, and handed it to him.

John B. laid the folder on his desk and opened it. He rummaged through it. It didn't take him long to locate what he was looking for.

"I'll be damned," he said. "I thought this might be the case. Look here, Carolyn."

She leaned over and looked. "My, my."

I sat there waiting for them to let me in on it, although I thought I already knew what they were going to say.

John B. looked up. "This is my contract with Percy Segal. He signed it right here in this office," he said, putting a finger on the papers in front of him. "Here's your check."

He laid the check on top of the contract and slid both of them over to me.

I took the contract and check and compared the signatures. I'm not a handwriting expert, but I was good enough for this job. A sixth-grader would have been good enough.

"They look anything alike to you?" John B. said.

"Not even close," I told him.

Chapter 5

"You're damn' right it's not even close," John B. said. "What the hell's going on here, Stephens?"

I was pretty sure we weren't friends anymore, and I hadn't even done anything.

"Don't ask me," I told him. "I'm just as much in the dark as you are."

And that was the truth. Don Cogsdill and I had assumed that the checks had been endorsed by the claimants, who'd pocketed the money. Obviously that hadn't been correct, at least in one case, and it proved once again that, for someone in my business, making assumptions was a bad thing to do. I knew better, but I'd slipped up. It was good that I'd found out, before things had gone any further.

It also made me realize that I'd better check something else, something I should have done before. I took out my list of claimants and pushed it over to John B. While he was looking at it, I said, "Are you the attorney for any of those men other than Percy Segal?"

I knew the answer, but I wanted him to confirm it.

He didn't take long to do it. "I am. In fact, I've represented several of them on one thing or another over the years. Maybe all of them. I'd have to check to be sure."

"Everyone on that list had checks mailed to themselves at this address," I said. "All twelve of them."

John B. slapped the list down on the desk. Carolyn gave a

startled jerk, and John B. said, "Dammit all, I want to know what's going on."

His face was red, and I wondered if he had high blood pressure.

"I'd like to know, too," I said. "I think it would be a good idea to check as many of those signatures as I could against the ones on any contracts you might have."

He gave the list to Carolyn and told her to pull the files on as many as she could find. She went to the filing cabinets, and John B. sat and seethed. Or pretended to. I looked out the window. The fly I'd seen earlier had gone, or maybe it had just died and fallen to the beige carpet. I didn't see it on the floor, but it was small, and I was a fair distance from the window.

In a few minutes Carolyn put a stack of the olive-colored folders on John B.'s desk. He started going through them, taking out contracts and folding them so that only the final page showed. Then he laid them on the desk.

I took the rest of the canceled checks from my briefcase and started to compare the signatures. Not a one of them on the checks bore even a faint resemblance to the ones on the contracts. Whoever had made the endorsements hadn't even tried to duplicate the person's actual signature. I figured that meant that the signer, whoever it was, hadn't had access to the contracts. Either that, or he just didn't care. Quite possibly he never thought anybody would be making a comparison. And he'd have been right, at least up until this moment. I was beginning to think that Mississippi Vivian had made a good point when she'd said I wasn't much of an investigator.

I know it's sexist to say this next thing, but that's just the way it is. The handwriting on all the signatures looked to me as if it was that of a man. It was big and awkward and sloppy, and I couldn't think of any women whose handwriting looked remotely like it.

Not that it meant anything special if the checks had been endorsed by a man. If Carolyn or Kathy had received the checks, she could have had a man sign them for her. Also, I didn't think that John B., if he was the guilty party, would have been dumb enough to sign the checks himself. So I didn't bother to ask for a sample of their handwriting. That could come later if it was necessary.

For that matter, if Percy Segal himself had been cashing the checks, he would have been smart enough not to endorse them himself. He'd get someone else to do it for him and split the money. I suspected that's what had happened.

I let John B. have his contracts back, and I took my list of claimants, gathered up the checks, and put everything back into the briefcase.

There was something else about the contracts. None of them had anything to do with insurance claims. I pointed that out to John B., who said that, in matters of insurance claims, he'd never represented anyone except Segal. So the checks arriving at his office made even less sense than before.

"What are you going to do about this, Ted?" John B. asked, letting me know that we were friends again and that he was just as puzzled by everything as I was.

"I'm going to find out who's been cheating National Insurance out of its money," I said.

"That's all well and good, but I want to know who's been using me as a cover-up for their dirty work. I want you to let me know when you find out."

"I already have a client," I told him, wondering if he was protesting too much. "I'm sure we'll be talking again, though, and if there's anything I can tell you without compromising my client, I'll do it."

"That's fair enough," John B. said. "I'd appreciate it."

I stood up. "I'll be going now. Pleased to meet you, Ms. Lacy."

"My pleasure, Mr. Stephens."

I didn't think she meant it, but Southern women are often big on mannerly behavior. I gave them both a smile and got out of there.

Chapter 6

Back out on the hot street, I walked to my rental. A few other cars passed by, and I imagined that the drivers looked at me with suspicion if not outright hostility. Maybe I was just being paranoid, but if Mississippi Vivian was right, everybody in town knew what I was there for.

Except that even I was no longer sure what I was there for. What had seemed to be a simple affair had gotten a lot more complicated since I'd started looking into things. The men to whom the checks had been made out weren't the endorsers, which most likely meant that they weren't the ones who'd cashed the checks, either. The checks had been cashed all around town, at banks, a check-cashing service, a drugstore, a supermarket, just as they would've been had twelve different claimants cashed them. Or if someone who didn't want to be identified had done it.

There was a dead man in the mix, too. A suicide in a small town is a rare event, so when one of the twelve people on my list happened to be the suicide, my instinct told me that there was something wrong somewhere. I didn't know exactly what it was yet, but I planned to find out.

I had so many things to consider and so many people that I needed to question that I thought about calling Don Cogsdill and telling him I was going to need to put another man on the job. I thought better of it, however. One stranger in a small town was more than enough to stir things up. I wasn't ready to get things any more stirred up than they were already.

I put the briefcase in the trunk and got in the car. I got the air conditioner going as soon as I could and started back toward the motel, which was out on the edge of town. I'd passed the tractor place on my way into Losgrove, and I thought I might as well stop there and have a talk with Kathy Hull.

Parsons Tractor was a big, sprawling place, consisting of a cinder-block building attached to a long metal shed that sat at the back of a lot covered with parked tractors, most of them green and shiny John Deeres. I saw a couple of used Massey Fergusons, their gray and red paint faded and dull. An even older International sat back near one end of the shed, faded by the sun from red to almost pink.

Under the long shed, men were repairing tractors, and I heard the banging of metal against metal, the chugging of an air compressor, and a very loud radio tuned to a country station. I didn't recognize the song. At the end of the shed there was a huge oak tree that spread its shade out over the tin roof of the shed and part of the lot in front.

I went into the cinder-block building and felt a cool blast of conditioned air that mingled the smells of engine oil and gasoline. The concrete floor was dark with ground-in dirt and stained with oil and grease. Fluorescent lights gave the room a pale glow. A counter ran along the far side of the big room, with aisles behind it made up of shelves full of tractor parts leading back into darkness. A couple of parts clerks stood behind the counter, but they paid no attention to me when I came in. I guess I didn't look like the type who'd be needing a new head gasket for his John Deere. The radio was playing in here, too, but it wasn't nearly as loud as it had been outside.

At one end of the counter was an old office desk, scuffed and scarred from its years of use. The desk was covered with ledger books. Sitting behind it was a slender young woman with dark-brown hair, blue-green eyes, and a strong resemblance to Carolyn Lacy. She looked up from an open ledger when I headed her way.

"Kathy Hull?" I said.

"That's right. How can I help you?"

"My name's Ted Stephens," I told her, wondering if she already knew. "I'm a private investigator from Houston, Texas, and I've just been down at John B. Campbell's office talking to him and your mother. I was wondering if I could have a few minutes of your time."

"Have a seat," she said, nodding at a rickety old wooden chair with a woven cane bottom that sagged in the middle.

I sat down and briefly told her what the situation was.

She thought it over for a little while, staring at the wall behind me. I was tempted to turn around to see what she was looking at, if anything, but I didn't. It was hung with fan belts and such, which were of no interest to me.

The two young men behind the counter talked and joked and paid no attention to either of us. Or at least I thought they didn't. One of them might have glanced our way, but I wasn't sure, and he went right back to joking with his buddy when I glanced in his direction.

"All right," Kathy said finally. "I think I understand what you've told me. What do you want to know from me?"

"I'd like to know if you ever saw any checks addressed to Percy Segal come across your desk on Fridays when you were at John B.'s office. Or to any of these other men."

I pulled the list of claimants from my pocket and read her the names. She listened until I was finished, and I expected her to say that she hadn't seen letters addressed to any of them. But she fooled me.

She changed the subject.

"Why on earth did the insurance company send the letters to

John B.'s office?" she said.

"The men asked the company to do it," I said, wondering if she was related to Mississippi Vivian. Surely Vivian would have mentioned it, however.

"Why would they do that?" she said.

I told her that was one of the things I'd like to find out.

"The men I know on that list don't live in the best part of town," she said. "I've heard of people out there getting their Social Security checks stolen right out of their mailboxes. Maybe that's why."

"It could be that way," I said, wondering why she'd bother making excuses for them. "I really don't know."

"Do you have any proof that those men asked for the letters to be mailed to John B.'s office?"

"We have letters from all of them making that request."

I thought about those letters now, for the first time, really, and wondered who had signed them. I hadn't seen them, but Don Cogsdill had told me they were on file. I had a feeling that the signatures might not have belonged to the person to whom the checks were made out.

"Did John B. know about the letters?" she said.

"He told me that he didn't. He said he'd never seen any of them come to his office."

"Then he didn't. John B.'s an honest man."

I thought about an old, old joke, one I'd first heard as a kid, the one about a man who sees a tombstone inscribed with the words, "Here Lies a Lawyer and an Honest Man." After thinking about the inscription for a minute, the man turns to a friend and says, "How come they bury folks two to a grave around here?"

I didn't think Kathy would appreciate the joke, so I didn't share it with her. Besides, she'd probably heard it long ago. And people never like my jokes, anyway.

"What about my mother?" Kathy said.

"What about her?"

"I mean, did she see the letters?"

"She says she didn't."

"Then she didn't. She always tells the truth."

It was nice to see a young woman with so much faith in her mother.

"So there wouldn't be any need to give her a lie-detector test," Kathy continued. "In fact, I wouldn't let her take one. I've read about them, and I don't like what I've heard. I don't want her humiliated that way. I'll take one, though, if I have to."

I wondered if she'd recognized my name, maybe read something about me in the newspapers. In a couple of my cases involving prominent people, I'd used lie-detector tests to prove guilt or innocence, and I believe in them. So she was way ahead of me, or thought she was. She was smart enough to know that her mother was likely to be a suspect in the check-cashing scheme and that she was likely to be one as well. Otherwise, I wouldn't have been there talking to her. But she wasn't quite as smart as she believed herself to be.

"Are you all through now?" I said. "Or do you have some more things to tell me?"

She grinned and shook her head. "I guess I got a little carried away. I'm through."

"Good. First of all we need to get something straight. I'm not asking you to take a lie-detector test, not now, anyway. Is that understood?"

"Sure. It's your investigation."

"I'm glad to hear it. So don't worry about the lie detector."

She shrugged. "I didn't say I was worried. I just don't want my mother to take one."

"I don't plan to ask her to." I didn't mention that plans can be changed. "Now can I ask you a few questions?"

"Go right ahead."

"All right. Here's the first question. When you go in on Friday afternoons to Joe B.'s office, is the mail on the desk waiting for you?"

"Sometimes it is. Sometimes it comes later."

"But it's always put on the desk? There's no mailbox?"

"The postman just puts it on the desk. Joe B. doesn't need a mailbox."

"And if it's there on the desk when you come in on Fridays, nobody goes through it until you get there?"

"Not that I know of."

"What about John B.?"

"He doesn't like dealing with the mail. That's one of the reasons he has me come in."

"Is he married? What about his wife?"

She looked at me with her blue-green eyes. "Didn't you tell me that you were a private investigator?"

I nodded.

"Then you should have found out that John B.'s wife died three years ago. Breast cancer. It really got him down. He got lonesome living by himself, and he missed his wife. He didn't like being around the place without her, so he sold his house and moved into the office."

I hadn't seen any living quarters, so I asked about them.

"There's an apartment with a little kitchen right there in the building," Kathy said. "It's beside John B.'s office."

I remembered the closed door next to the office. John B. must have been living in a Spartan style. I figured he ate a lot of meals at the Magnolia Café. Or maybe he was a gourmet cook. It didn't matter one way or the other.

I had some more questions to ask, but this wasn't the time. I'd stirred up enough trouble for one day, and I needed to think over all the things I'd learned.

Kathy and her mother would have plenty to talk about that evening, and John B. might even talk about it with them if he didn't spend all his time watching TV in his lonely bachelor room. Or cooking gourmet meals. I thanked Kathy for her time and started to leave.

Before I could get to the door, one of the men behind the counter came around the end of it and caught up with me. He put a big, hairy-knuckled hand on my shoulder to stop me, so I turned to look at him. He dropped his hand as I turned.

He was bigger than I'd thought he was, not as tall as me but bigger across the shoulders. He was also a lot younger than I'd thought, probably not more than twenty. He had on a green John Deere cap, and he had a toothpick stuck in the corner of his mouth. He was smiling, but I didn't think he meant it.

"What?" I said.

He spit the toothpick on the floor, which I considered poor hygiene. It didn't speak well for his upbringing, either.

"You got a problem with Kathy?" he said.

"No."

He moved forward and bumped me lightly with his shoulder. "Looked to me like you did."

He was not only more than twenty years younger than I was. He was about ten times as dumb.

"You ought not to pick on an old man," I told him. "You should respect your elders. One of these days you'll be as old and feeble as I am."

He nodded as if he could see that I was elderly, but I could tell he didn't believe the part about how someday he'd be as old as I was.

"We're kind of old-fashioned," I said. "My wife and me. She doesn't have a job, so she kind of depends on the income I bring in. It wouldn't do if you were to put me in the hospital."

"You're sure a mouthy old fart," he said. "We don't need you coming around here and bothering us."

"Us?" I said. "I didn't even talk to you until you put your hand on me."

He laughed. "What? You didn't like that? Too damn' bad. I do what I please to old wussies like you."

I try never to get into fights with the young and stupid, and I'd been holding onto my temper pretty well up until that point. It was bad enough that he was accusing me of bothering Kathy when I'd done no such thing, and it was even worse when he'd put his hand on me, but I'd been willing to let that pass. I didn't see any need for causing a real problem in town before I'd really gotten started on my investigation. But he shouldn't have called me a name on top of everything else.

I lifted my right foot and slid the hard edge of my shoe sole down his calf before I stomped on his arch.

His eyes bugged out in surprise. He couldn't believe an old wussie would do that to him. He might even have had the idea that he could retaliate, maybe even hurt me pretty badly.

Maybe he could have, if I'd given him the chance, which I didn't. I hit him in the sternum with my right fist, middle knuckle extended. Not too hard. Just hard enough.

He staggered back a couple of steps, trying to get his breath. While he was doing that, I went over to Kathy's desk, got the chair, and carried it over to where he was gasping. I put the chair down behind him, then went around in front of him. His eyes were still a little bugged out, so I pushed him down onto the chair.

He sat down, bulging the already drooping cane bottom, and said, "You . . . uh . . . better . . . get on . . . out of here."

By that time Kathy was standing beside me. "Johnny Turner, you ought to be ashamed of yourself. What if this gentleman had been a customer?"

"He don't look . . . uh . . . like a customer."

"Don't judge a book by its cover," I said. "That's what my mother always told me."

He gave me a nasty look. Just another clue that he didn't have much respect for his elders. I don't know what's gotten into people these days. I blame their upbringing.

"I'm sorry, Mr. Stephens," Kathy said. "I don't know what got into Johnny."

I knew, I thought. Johnny was sweet on her and wanted to impress her. He'd done that, I thought, but maybe not the way he'd planned it.

"That's all right," I said, waving my hand in dismissal to show what a good sport I was. "And call me Ted. I hope I didn't hurt him."

The look he'd given me before was mild compared to the one I got that time. I smiled at him, to show I didn't hold it against him.

"Thanks again for your help, Kathy," I said. "I might have a few more questions later on if that wouldn't be too much of a bother."

"It wouldn't be a bother," she said, and poor Johnny glared at me so hard I thought he might pull a hernia.

I was still grinning when I went out the door.

Chapter 7

I thought I deserved a break, so I went to the motel. I pitched the briefcase on the bed and turned on the TV. A talking head was reading a story about the death of some celebrity I'd never heard of.

The truth is, it would have been hard for them to talk about a celebrity I *had* heard of. I don't follow the movies. I don't listen to the radio often, and I don't watch much TV. I just turn them on for background noise. I don't read much past the front page of a newspaper, except for the crime news.

I sat in the only chair in the room, an uncomfortable armchair, and propped my feet up on the bed while I thought over what I'd learned since I'd arrived in Losgrove. It was a lot, but instead of helping me get the case solved and get back to Houston, it had just complicated things.

Number one on the list of complications was the death of Percy Segal. If he'd just had the good grace to have a heart attack, I wouldn't have worried much about it, but suicide with a rifle?

Shot in the chest?

I haven't had a lot of experience with suicides, but I've had enough to know that people who take their own lives rarely seem to choose a rifle to do the job. And when they do use a rifle, they don't shoot themselves in the chest. Too uncertain. You might just end up wounding yourself badly, or bleeding to death, which is no way to go, not for someone who wants a fast exit.

And I'd never heard of someone killing himself in another man's house. That just didn't sound right, unless Segal had been carrying some grudge against Wade Dickie.

Segal was right at the top of my suspect list for the check scam now, even if he was dead. Obviously I was going to have to talk to the sheriff about the suicide, unless I could get things taken care of without bothering him. After all, investigating Segal's murder wasn't in my job description. I have to admit that I was curious about it, however, and I thought it might very well end up being connected to my investigation, though right now I couldn't see how.

I was even more curious about those checks arriving at John B.'s office without anybody knowing about them. I just didn't believe that part of the story. Somebody knew. Either John B., Kathy, or Carolyn had to have known.

Eventually, I'd find out. If you talk to people long enough, and if you know how to talk to them, you can find out just about anything. It takes a little patience, but I have plenty of that. You don't last very long as a private investigator without it.

After I'd thought things over for a while, I turned off the TV and used the room phone to place a long-distance call to my wife, to see how things were going at home and to let her know I loved her. One of our problems a few years earlier had been the separations caused by my job when I'd been a cop. We were separated even more now, but she didn't seem to mind quite as much. She understood that I had to go out of town on cases, and she knew I'd get home as soon as I could.

At least I hoped she did.

Sarah sounded happy when she answered the phone, and she told me that she'd been messing around in the yard most of the day, pulling weeds out of the flowerbeds and such. I've never been able to understand what kind of pleasure a person could get from that kind of activity, but she loves it, so I don't question it. It does my heart good to hear her voice when she's happy because I know things are going to be fine with us.

"When are you coming home?" she asked me after we'd talked for a couple of minutes.

"This might take longer than I thought," I told her. "Things are a little more complicated than they were supposed to be."

"You've met a woman, haven't you."

I laughed because I knew she was joking. There'd been a time when she might not have been able to make a joke like that, but now she knew very well that I'd never done more than look at another woman during all the years we'd been married. Since it was a joke, I decided to play along.

"Yes," I said. "There's a woman. Her name is Mississippi Vivian."

"With a name like that she must be a cheap floozy."

Sarah talks like that sometimes, as if she were a character in some bad movie from fifty or sixty years ago. I think she just does it for fun, but I've never been sure.

"She's a waitress," I said.

"A waitress can be a floozy. It's not likely, but it's possible."

"Not this one," I said, and I told her about Mississippi Vivian.

"You meet some interesting people," she said when I was through.

The way she said *interesting,* I knew she meant *strange.* I had to agree with her.

"That's part of what makes the job so much fun," I said.

"Some people would call it work."

"Not me," I said. "It's pure fun."

And it was. I enjoyed all of it: questioning people, uncovering their motives, untangling the crooked webs they'd woven for themselves, and finally getting the information that would lead me to the closing of the case.

"Well, don't have too much fun without me," Sarah said.

"It's always more fun when you're around," I told her, and that was the truth. I hoped she believed it.

We talked a little longer, and I told her I had to go because it was about time for dinner at the local café."

"And who will your waitress be?"

"Mississippi Vivian," I said. "If I'm lucky."

Unfortunately, Vivian didn't work a twelve-hour shift, and she wasn't on duty when I went back to the Magnolia Café. The waitress who'd taken her place was named Gladys, and she looked nothing like Vivian. If she was even out of high school, it was only by a month or so. I asked her about Vivian. She might have gotten the mistaken idea that I was interested in asking Vivian out. Sometimes people misunderstand me. It's a gift I have.

"You don't think she'd eat *here*, do you?" Gladys said. "She likes to go to Hamburger Heaven now and then. You might catch her there."

"Where's Hamburger Heaven?"

"Two streets over. You can't miss it."

She was right about that. There were only four streets in the Losgrove business district. It was hard to get lost. I thanked her and left. I'd been hoping to sample the Magnolia's dinner menu, but I was willing to settle for a hamburger if that was what I had to do to talk to Mississippi Vivian again.

Hamburger Heaven looked a little like a Dairy Queen from the outside, but then so did a lot of other hamburger joints that hoped to get some of the DQ business. Their owners knew a good thing when they saw one, and they didn't mind being thought of as copycats. I could smell onion rings and french fries before I even opened the door.

Mississippi Vivian was sitting in a booth by herself, working on something I couldn't identify, although it looked a little like a hamburger. I sat down uninvited and asked what it was.

"Why?" she said. "You thinking about getting one?"

I thought of the man who'd asked about the pie that morning. I should have known she wouldn't tell me what she was eating.

"I won't know if I want it until you tell me what it is," I said.

She put it down in the plastic basket in front of her. "What does it look like?"

It looked like a hamburger patty between two fried corn tacos.

"Some kind of hamburger," I said. "But it's not a hamburger."

"It's a tacoburger. It doesn't have as much starch as a hamburger. No buns."

I looked at the fries in the basket. She noticed the direction of my gaze.

"I didn't say I was cutting down on starches. I was just telling you about the tacoburger. You gonna get one?"

I nodded and went to the counter to order. I got a Pepsi along with my receipt and went back to the table.

"You didn't just happen to drop in here, did you?" Vivian said.

"No. I thought we might have another talk."

"About what?"

She took a big bite of her tacoburger. The crisp tacos crackled when she bit into it.

I took a drink of my Pepsi. It was a little watery, but I didn't mind.

"I want to know something about the mail delivery here in Losgrove," I said. "John B. told me that the postman just drops the mail on a desk when he brings it by the law office. I thought that was a little unusual."

"I don't see anything unusual about it," she said when she'd finished chewing. "That's the way it is around here."

"I thought most businesses in small towns had a post-office box," I said, hoping that might get me an answer.

"Not here," she said. She tore open a ketchup packet and squeezed ketchup out onto the paper in the basket. She tossed the packet aside and dipped a fry in the ketchup. "Most people get their mail at home or at their place of business. I don't think anybody except maybe the tractor place and the lumberyard has a box at the post office. Boxes cost money. Who'd have a box when they could get the mail delivered right to their door for free?"

She bit the end off the fry and dipped what was left into the ketchup. What she'd said made sense, but it still seemed a little odd to me.

"Who delivers the mail here in town?" I asked.

Naturally she didn't answer me directly. She said, "Why do you want to know that?"

I was getting used to her by now. I said, "Since you're an employee of the company now, I'm going to tell you why I want to know, but you can't tell anyone else."

"As an employee of the company, do I have to pay withholding on the money you gave me?"

"That was just between us. You can do whatever you want to about it. It's cash money, and I'm not going to report it."

She nodded. "When do I get paid again?"

"We'll discuss that later."

She seemed satisfied with that, and I was about to tell her why I wanted to know who delivered the mail when my number was called. I went over to the counter and got my tacoburger and fries. When I sat back down, I tried the burger. For a second, things were fine. Then my mouth started to burn. I swallowed and took a big drink of the watery Pepsi.

When I could talk again, I said, "Why didn't you warn me about the jalapenos?"

"You didn't ask me."

I wasn't sure she'd have told me even if I'd asked. I took another drink. Jalapenos weren't good for my delicate stomach.

"Besides," she said, "I thought you'd know. It's a tacoburger, after all."

"I never ate one before."

I took the top taco off and scraped some of the jalapenos onto a napkin.

"I hope you'll be all right," Vivian said.

"I'll be fine. But never mind. Let me tell you why I'm here in Losgrove and what the mail has to do with it."

I ran through the case for her as quickly as I could, now and then taking a bite of the tacoburger and hoping I hadn't missed too many of the jalapenos. When I was finished explaining things, she didn't say anything for a while. She finished her tacoburger, and I did the same. I needed a refill on the Pepsi to do it, though.

"All those men you mentioned," Vivian said when we were both through eating. "I don't think they're hurt. They sure haven't ever showed any sign of it. Most of them have jobs. A couple of them play on the church softball team."

I didn't have to ask her which church she was talking about, and I wasn't surprised at all by what she'd told me. Well, maybe the church part was surprising, but not the fact that the men had jobs and didn't seem to be injured.

"What about the mail carrier?" I said. "And I'd like to know something about the postmaster, too."

She was interested now, and she came right out with the answer. "We just have a few postmen in town. Al Corley and Tom Sturdivant have carried the mail here as long as I can remember. They're both in their sixties and probably about to retire. Roy Welling is younger, though. Aubrey Stokes is the postmaster. He's been here just as long as Al and Tom. They're all good men. I don't think they'd be the type to be involved in anything criminal."

I could have told her that hardly anybody who's involved in something criminal seems to be the type. I've met burglars who you might take for priests and killers you might think were choirboys.

"I'm sure they're fine folks," I said, "but in my line of work, you have to check up on everybody. It's just part of the job."

Mississippi Vivian said she understood, and maybe she did. It didn't really matter, one way or the other.

"What about the sheriff?" I said.

"His name's Joe Bronte."

I was pretty sure she knew that wasn't what I meant. I said, "You told me that already."

"I did? Well, he's been sheriff for a long time so the voters must like him."

That wasn't what I meant, either, so I tried again.

"Sometimes the voters like a crook because he does them favors."

Vivian shook her head. "Joe wouldn't do that."

"So if I went to him and laid out my case and explained why I'm here, I could trust him to keep his mouth shut and help me, just the way you're doing."

"I think so. You wouldn't even have to pay him. In fact, you better not even try. Joe's honest, and he might think you were bribing him. Not that he always follows the law. He doesn't. Nothing wrong with that, though, long as justice gets done."

I nodded. I understood how things were done in small towns and backwoods counties. It worked all right as long as the sheriff was honest, but there were times when the power went to a man's head and turned him into something worse than the lowest criminal. I'd dealt with someone like that once, and I hoped I wouldn't have to again.

We were both finished with our tacoburgers and fries. I gathered up the stray paper and ketchup packets, stuffed them in the plastic baskets that had held our burgers, and carried the baskets to the trash. There was a sign on the bin that said, "Please Do Not Put Plastic Basket's in the Trash." I thought about giving someone a lecture on the use of the apostrophe, but I didn't know who'd be the right person. I put the papers in the trash, set the baskets on top of the bin, and went back to where Mississippi Vivian was sipping her drink. I had a little of the Pepsi refill left, so I took a drink, myself.

"What do you mean about the sheriff not following the law?" I said when I was finished.

She thought about it and then told me a little story.

"One time old Ham Wilson got drunk. Not that it was unusual for Ham to be drunk. He was drunk about as often as he was sober, or maybe more often, but usually he stayed at home when he was in bad shape. Kept out of trouble that way. This time, though, he must have been out of sardines because he was at the Safeway, filling his pockets up with those little flat cans of them. Somebody saw him and called the sheriff. When Joe got there, Ham was trying to sneak past the cashier." She paused. "I heard later he must've had fifteen cans of sardines in his pockets. Anyway, Joe didn't file any charges on him. Instead of taking him to jail, he paid for a couple of cans of sardines, took Ham home, and had some sardines and crackers with him. Then he got him sobered up. That's the way Joe operates. He does what he thinks is right, even if that's not always exactly what the law says."

Bronte sounded like the kind of man I could work with and not one of the power-hungry kind. I wasn't sure I could trust him, but I'd decide that later, after I'd talked to him.

I told Vivian that we'd chat again, and I left, tossing the Pepsi cup into the trash bin as I passed by.

Chapter 8

Back at the motel I took a long shower to wash away some of the Mississippi grit I'd accumulated during the day and then stretched out on the bed in my underwear. The mattress was thin, but then this wasn't exactly a luxury suite. I didn't mind. I could sleep on the floor if I had to. I'd slept on hard ground and been happy.

I thought things over for a few minutes, then got on the phone and dialed the operator for long distance. I called my old friend Frank Briscoe, who until recently had been the district attorney in Houston. He'd decided to run for congress, however, so he'd given up the position of DA. Our buddy Carol Vance was going to have that job, but it would be three weeks before he took office.

When I told Frank who was calling, he said, "Ted Stephens, you sorry son of a bitch, if I've told you once, I've told you a hundred times not to call me at home. I have things to do. Books to read, TV shows to watch. Card games to play. I have a family. I don't have time to take calls from come cheap-ass private eye."

"I'm calling long distance," I said. "From Mississippi."

"I don't care if you're calling from Carnaby Street. I'm going to hang up now, and don't call me back."

I knew he didn't really mean it. Frank always talks like that, and I never let it bother me. Besides, I can give as well as I get.

"Look, you out-of-work shyster," I said, "you won't be going to congress if I don't give you some help. In fact, I already have. So if you hang up on me, I'll help your opponent instead of you, and I'll tell everybody about you and that goat you thought was so sexy. You won't be going to congress. You'll be locked up in the jail downtown so fast it'll make your head swim."

"That's a vile slander," Frank said. "That was no goat you caught me with. It was a sheep, and you know it, you damned wiretapper."

I laughed. It was hard to get the better of Frank. I'd been helping him a little to prepare for his campaign, digging the dirt on his opponent, and there was plenty of dirt to dig. Frank wouldn't have to use even the half of what I'd found out so far. It wasn't as spicy as getting caught romancing a goat, or even a sheep, but it was spicy enough.

Of course the other side was digging the dirt on Frank, too, and he had plenty of enemies. One of the editorial writers for a community paper had done a column when Frank announced that he was running for congress and had called him a *jackass.* In another editorial a week or so later, the same guy called me a *lackey* and a *wiretapper,* which is where Frank had come up with that one.

Frank was outraged at the columnist for what he'd said about him, and he was just as outraged at what had been said about me. We had a friend named Joe Jamail, who was a high-powered civil lawyer, and Frank wanted to hire him to sue the paper for libel on behalf of both of us. I told him I didn't want to be a party to any such lawsuit. I told him that while I wasn't anybody's lackey, I wasn't absolutely sure that any lawyer, no matter how good he was, could prove I hadn't ever tapped a wire. Added to that, I said, I was doubtful that even Daniel Webster himself could prove that Frank wasn't a jackass.

Frank had laughed about that. What he'd failed to mention to me, however, was that he'd already telephoned his lawyer friend and asked him about taking the case. The lawyer had told me about it later and said that he'd just about exploded while he tried to hold in his laughter. He'd let Frank down too easily, though, which is why Frank had called me. He'd hoped that with me backing him up, the lawyer would change his mind and take the case.

It didn't happen, and I'd agreed that I'd keep on working for Frank as long as he didn't ask me to tap any wires or kiss his ass like a lackey. Frank had promised I wouldn't have to do either one, and I'd stayed on with him. So I figured he owed me a favor.

"What kind of a favor?" he said when I told him.

"I'm working a case in Mississippi," I said.

"I can't do anything for you if you're in Mississippi. I'm in Houston, and I'm not even the DA here anymore, much less in Mississippi. So I don't think I can help you."

"You haven't even heard what it is I want you to help me with."

"You said it was in Mississippi. That's all I need to hear."

"No it's not. It's tied to Houston, and the crimes are against a Houston firm, National Insurance."

"Well," Frank said, "that might make a difference."

"I thought it might. I have a bunch of insurance claimants who say they got hurt while working on the docks in Houston, hurt so bad that they're disabled. They're all collecting on policies from National. Every one of them is from Losgrove, Mississippi, and they're all living back here now. Some of them, maybe all of them, have jobs they couldn't handle if they were injured the way they claim to be. Some of them are playing softball on a church team. And I think maybe some kind of kickback to the union bosses could be involved, too."

"You *think*," Frank said. "You got any proof on any of this?"

I admitted that I didn't have any proof, not yet.

"But you know me," I said. "I'll get the proof if it's there to be gotten."

"Probably get it by tapping some poor old boy's telephone."

"You going to start writing editorials for that reporter pal of yours?"

"Just making a comment, and he's not my pal. I was just joking. No need for you to take offense."

"I'm not taking offense. I was joking, too. Are you going to do anything for me, or not?"

"*If* you can prove that there have been crimes committed and *if* they were committed in Houston," Frank said, "and that's a mighty big *if,* then Carol Vance will take the cases, no question about it. That is, he'll take the ones about the false claims. I think the kickbacks to the union bosses, if there are any, would be a federal crime. Nothing there for us local boys."

I hadn't thought of that. Now that he'd mentioned it, I was pretty sure he was right, but that didn't make any difference. As far as I was concerned, the kickbacks, if they existed, didn't have anything to do with National Insurance, and that was who I worked for.

"Why don't you let Carol know what I'm working on," I said. "He might appreciate a little advance warning."

"You're always getting me to do your job for you, Stephens. But I'll give him a call. He wouldn't be where he is, if it weren't for you and me."

I thanked him, and then he said, "You need to remember that Carol doesn't take office for three weeks. He can't do anything until then."

"I'll keep that in mind," I said, and I thanked him again.

"Never mind thanking me," he said. "How about something a little more substantial?"

"More substantial? Like what?"

"Like a handsome contribution to my campaign fund. A man

can't get elected these days unless he has a sizeable war chest. You know that."

I laughed. "I've already worked for you for nothing, been called a lackey and a wiretapper, and now you're asking me for money? This is business we're talking here, Frank. It's not about your campaign. I'll say one thing for you, though. You've got more nerve than a government mule."

"Does that mean I can't expect a contribution?"

"I gave at the office."

"Are you sure?" Frank said.

"I'm sure."

"Well, don't think I'm not going to check our records and see."

"Frank," I said, "you're about the most aggravating man I know."

"You don't know yourself very well, then," he said, and he hung up.

I should've known he wouldn't let me have the last word.

CHAPTER 9

After talking to Frank, I turned the TV back on. The dead celebrity was still getting all the coverage, so I was about to turn off the set when someone knocked at the door. I wondered who it could be. I knew it wasn't the maid coming by to do a turndown or to bring me a mint for my pillow. This wasn't that kind of place. Maybe it was the bug exterminator.

I walked over to the door. There was no peephole, so I said, "Who is it?"

"Kathy Hull," came the answer. "Can I come in and talk to you?"

"Sure," I said, "but give me a minute."

I hated to make her wait outside, but I didn't think it would be a good idea to meet with her while I was wearing nothing but my tightie whities. I put on my shirt, pants, and shoes, then went to the door and opened it.

There she stood, looking at me with those blue-green eyes. She'd been home after work and put on fresh clothes and makeup. She smelled good, too. I thought it was a good thing I'd never be tempted by anyone other than Sarah, because Ms. Hull was very attractive indeed.

"May I come in?" she said.

"Please do," I told her, stepping aside and holding the door open. "I don't have much to offer in the way of comfort. You take the chair, and I'll sit on the bed."

She went to the chair and sat down.

"Can I offer you something to drink?" I said.

She gave me a quizzical look. "This is a dry county."

"Not that kind of drink. I have Coke and 7-Up. Name your poison."

She looked around the room. "I don't see a refrigerator."

"There's a cold-drink machine around the corner. I'm buying."

"Well," she said, "in that case, I'll take a Coke."

I left the room and went to the machine, which was cranky and taking only the correct change. Luckily, I had just enough, so I bought her a Coke and myself a 7-Up. When I got back to the room, Kathy was watching the TV as if she might be interested in the dead celebrity.

I asked her if she minded if I turned the set off. She said she didn't, so I walked over and turned off the TV. I opened her drink can and poured most of the Coke into one of the plastic glasses the motel provided. I prefer to drink straight from the can. All those stories about how you can catch some kind of disease from rat urine on drink cans are greatly exaggerated, if you ask me.

I settled myself on the bed, took a sip of the 7-Up and said, "Thanks for stopping by to see me. It gets kind of lonesome with only the TV for company. But I don't think you came just to cheer up a lonely old man."

She looked around for somewhere to set her drink, but there wasn't anywhere. She held it in her lap with both hands. I wondered if she might actually be there to try to tempt me. It wouldn't work, but it was kind of pleasant to think that she might try.

"Look, Mr. Stephens," she began, and I knew that she wasn't interested in tempting me.

I can't say I wasn't at least a little bit disappointed, but it was for the best, and I decided to make sure she knew it.

"I might be old enough to be your daddy, but I think we should be on a first-name basis if we're going to have a friendly talk. Call me Ted."

"All right, Ted. What makes you think I didn't come by just to welcome a stranger to our little city?"

"Because that's not the way things work. You have a lot better things to do than that. Even in a small town there are a lot of things more fun than talking to an old man in a motel room."

She looked down at her Coke. "You met my mother today, Ted. Did you like her?"

I wondered for a second if Kathy was going to try her hand at matchmaking, sort of tempting me at second hand. It didn't seem likely, but you never know what some people might do.

"She seemed like a nice woman," I said. "Smart. Good at her job. John B. trusts her completely, I'd say."

Kathy looked up as if I'd finally said the right thing. "John B. does trust her. So do I. So would anybody who knew her. That would include just about everybody in town, and I don't want anything to change that."

So that was it. She was here to impress me with what a fine upstanding citizen her mother was, a pillar of the community, not at all the kind of person who might meddle with mail that she was entrusted with.

"I don't plan to try changing the way people feel about your mother," I said.

"That's not what I mean, exactly."

I waited to see if she'd tell me what she did mean, exactly. It took a couple of seconds, but she finally came out with it.

"I don't want you to cause my mother any problems while you're here."

As far as I knew, I hadn't caused Carolyn Lacy any problems, and so far I didn't have any reason to try causing any. But maybe Kathy knew something I wasn't aware of. Maybe she was going to start up about the lie detector again.

"If you're talking about John B.'s mail and who might have gone through it," I said, "then I don't consider your mother a suspect right now."

That wasn't strictly true. Everybody I'd met was a suspect except for Mississippi Vivian, but I didn't have any evidence to make me believe that Carolyn had been doing anything wrong. Not yet, anyway. Someone had been doing something wrong. I was sure of that. But that was about all I was sure about in this case.

"On the other hand," I said, "if you know something that I don't, this would be as good a time as any to talk about it."

Kathy tensed, and her voice was strained when she spoke. "I don't know anything at all about your investigation, whatever it is. I'm glad to hear my mother's not a suspect, and she'd better never become one. She never did anything with John B.'s mail, and she doesn't know anything about those checks. That's the truth."

Well, maybe it was, and maybe it wasn't. It was nice of Kathy to defend her mother, though. Lots of young people these days wouldn't take the trouble. They don't care about their parents as much as they should.

"I believe you," I said.

I say things like that all the time, even when I don't mean them. Some people might consider them lies, but it's all part of the game. People lie to me, and I lie to them. Now and then it was hard to say who lied the most, but I like to think that my own lies are in the service of some kind of justice, whereas their lies are used to cover up the truth. That's not to say that Kathy was lying about anything. As far as I knew, she was a beacon of truth.

She took a drink of her Coke and looked at me over the rim of the glass, those blue-green eyes assessing me. I looked as innocent as I could, which is pretty innocent. I've had a lot of practice. When she lowered the glass, she said, "I'm glad you believe me. My mother would never do anything dishonest or wrong."

"I'm sure you're right." I paused. "Would it be okay if we changed the subject now?"

Kathy nodded and tried a smile. She managed about half of one.

"Good," I said. "There's something I'd like to ask you if you don't mind."

She did the half smile again. "Go right ahead."

She didn't sound eager, but I didn't mind that. I didn't need any encouragement.

"I'm looking into a few things for the company I work for," I said. "I have a list of people that I'm checking on. I think some of them might be working for you at the tractor place. I'd like to drop by there tomorrow and have a look at your records, just to verify their employment. After I do, I might have a couple of questions about the kind of work they do there."

Kathy stood up and walked over to the little nightstand by the bed. She set her glass down by the clock radio with its red glowing numbers. It was nine-ten.

"The people who work at the tractor company are good people," she said.

From what I was hearing from her and Mississippi Vivian, Losgrove, Mississippi, must have been a little like Shangri-La. Nobody in it but good people.

"I'm sure they are," I said. "You take that Johnny Turner. He's a fine young man, no doubt about it, but he didn't mind picking a fight with an old fella like me."

"Johnny's been under some stress lately."

"What kind of stress?"

"It doesn't have anything to do with you or what you're looking into. And he doesn't work at the tractor place, anyway."

I could have asked how she could be certain Turner didn't have anything to do with my case, and later I might do that. But, at the moment, I wanted to talk about those employment records.

"I'm sorry to hear it," I said. "Anyway, let's get back to those records of yours. All I want to do is verify that certain people work at the tractor place. Johnny Turner's not one of them. I won't cause you any trouble."

"The people who work there are more than just good people," Kathy said. She walked to the door and put her hand on the knob before turning to look at me. "They're also loyal employees. They're loyal to the tractor place, and we're loyal to them."

I didn't see anything wrong with that. "That's the way it should be."

"True. And we want things to stay that way. Which is why you won't be allowed to look at those records. You can go to anybody you want to and try to get them, but those records are confidential, and they're going to stay that way."

She opened the door and left.

I sat on the bed and looked at the door. I hadn't drunk much of my 7-Up can, so I took a swallow. The soda was still cool, so I drank some more of it while I thought about what had just happened.

When I'd taken the case, I'd thought it would be a simple job, a few days out of town, a quick investigation, and I'd be back home in Houston.

It wasn't shaping up to be like that, however. I knew less now about what was going on than I had when I'd started. In fact, the more I found out, the less I knew. I'd been on cases like that before. They seldom turned out well.

Maybe this one would, I told myself, but I must not have been convincing because I didn't believe it even for a second.

Chapter 10

The next morning the first thing I did after I got myself shaved and ready for the day was to call the sheriff's department. It wasn't hard to find the number. I just used an old professional investigator's trick and looked in the phone book.

A man answered the phone, and I asked to speak to the sheriff.

"This is the sheriff," the man said.

Obviously he ran a small department or he wouldn't be answering the phone himself. I told him my name and asked if he knew who I was.

"I know who you are, all right. You've been bothering a few people here in town, so I called up Buster Kerns to ask about you."

Buster was the sheriff of Harris County, which includes Houston and a little more besides. I'd known him for a long time, and we'd worked a few cases together, me on the private side and him working for the public good. I'd even helped him out a time or two by letting him claim credit for a couple of them that I'd solved.

"I haven't been bothering anybody," I said.

"That's your story. Others feel a little differently."

I knew it wouldn't do any good to ask him what others he was talking about.

"I hope Buster gave me a good report," I said.

"He said you were good at your job, that you had a national

reputation, and that I could trust you completely. Up to a point."

"Good old Buster. I'll have to send him some flowers."

Bronte snorted. "He didn't strike me as the flower type. You might try candy instead."

"I'll keep it in mind. How about you? Would breakfast be all right?"

"I'll pick you up in fifteen minutes."

I started to tell him where I was staying. He said, "I know where you're staying. We're not just some hick-town department, you know."

"I didn't think you were. How about going to the Magnolia Café?"

"That's fine. We'll see what Vivian's throwing out this morning."

"I'll meet you out front," I said.

"Fifteen minutes," he repeated and hung up.

I walked around to the front of the motel to wait. It wasn't even eight o'clock yet, but the heat and humidity were already taking hold. I heard a mockingbird singing somewhere, but I couldn't see it. A couple of cars drove by, raising a little dust on the dry streets, but the drivers paid no attention to the man standing in front of the motel with a briefcase in his hand. As far as they were concerned, I might as well not have existed. That was fine with me. It meant I was feeling less paranoid this morning.

The sheriff pulled up in a white Ford Crown Vic a couple of years old. It had a light-bar on top and the department's insignia on the door in dark green.

I opened the door on the passenger side and looked in.

"Sheriff Bronte?" I said.

"That's me. Get in."

I tossed the briefcase in the seat, got in, and closed the door. Bronte took off. He didn't seem to be in a talking mood, so I looked him over without being obvious about it. People have a certain idea of what of a Southern sheriff should look like. He should be a big man, maybe two hundred and fifty pounds, most of it fat, and his belly should hide his belt buckle. He should have a pudgy red face with mean little eyes like a pig's. The stub of a cigar stuck in the corner of his mouth wouldn't be lit, and he'd be chewing on it.

Bronte didn't look like that at all. He was about five-ten or -eleven. It was hard to tell with him sitting down. He might have weighed a hundred and seventy-five with all his clothes on and soaking wet. His eyes weren't small at all, and they looked even bigger than they were because they were magnified by his gold-rimmed glasses. His straw Western-style hat was on the seat between us, so I could see that his thinning hair that had once been black was mostly gray. He didn't wear a uniform, just a Western-cut shirt, a pair of pressed khakis, and a pair of worn black shoes with thick rubber soles.

We rode to the café in silence except for the sound of the tires on the pavement. When we arrived, he parked the car and said, "Tell me what this is all about."

He left the engine running, so the air conditioner would keep us cool. I was grateful for that.

"By *this,* do you mean my investigation?"

"You know what I mean."

Of course I knew, but I wondered why he didn't know. He'd have been able to find out if he'd really wanted to. I figured he knew all right, but he wanted to hear it from me to be sure what he'd heard was accurate. Or to see if I'd tell him the truth. I didn't see any reason to hide anything, and it wouldn't have done any good, so I gave him a quick summary.

"I have three cases, I think. First, there's theft of checks from the mail, which would be a federal case. Then there's a little bit of fraud by way of filing false insurance claims. That's for the state to handle when I get it wrapped up. And, finally, it looks as if there's been some bribing of union officials. That might wind up being either a state or a federal case or both."

Bronte sat with both hands on the wheel, facing forward. He hadn't looked straight at me since I got in the car.

"That's all you got?"

"You don't think that's enough?"

"It's enough, all right. It all has to do with those local boys that went to Houston and took jobs on the docks, I guess."

"Yes, sir. It surely does."

"You can tell me more about it while we eat," he said. He turned off the engine and got out of the car.

I got out on my side and followed him into the restaurant. I smelled bacon as soon as we got inside and heard it sizzling on a grill. Mississippi Vivian came to meet us. Several people sat at the counter, and they all turned to look at us, but they turned back to their food pretty quickly.

"Morning, Sheriff," Vivian said. "Morning, Ted."

The sheriff looked at me quizzically when she spoke my first name. I just shrugged, and Vivian led us to the table where she and I had sat to talk. She asked if that would be okay.

"It's fine," I told her as I put my briefcase on the floor and sat down.

Bronte sat down across from me, and Vivian left.

"She's getting coffee," Bronte said, and sure enough, Vivian was back in a few seconds with a coffee cup in each hand. She set them down on the table, and Bronte looked up at her. "What do you have that's good this morning?"

I suppressed a groan because I knew what kind of answer, or non-answer, he'd get. Surely he knew Mississippi Vivian better than to ask her a question like that. Or maybe he did it just to aggravate her.

"Everything's good," she said. "You know that."

"I meant what's on the menu this morning."

"The breakfast menu's where it always is." She pointed to a blackboard. "That's what we have. Take your pick."

Bronte looked at the blackboard. So did I.

"Are the eggs fresh?" he said.

"I don't know where they got the eggs or when the chickens laid them. Do you want breakfast or not?"

"I guess I do," Bronte said. "Give me the usual."

The usual. He'd just been aggravating her all along.

"What's *the usual?*" I said.

"Heart attack on a plate," Bronte said. "That'd be number four on the blackboard."

I checked it out. Two eggs, any style, bacon, buttered toast, and grits with gravy.

"I'll have the same thing," I said.

"How do you want those eggs?" Vivian said.

"Scrambled."

"Hard or soft?"

"Medium."

"Joe likes his hot. You want yours the same?"

"Hot? You mean you're going to bring me eggs you cooked yesterday and kept in the refrigerator overnight?"

"That's not what I mean," Vivian said. "You want 'em hot or not?"

I knew she'd never tell me what she was talking about, no matter how many questions I asked, so I looked at Bronte.

"Hot means they put some picante sauce on mine," he said.

"My stomach won't take that," I said. "Jalapenos on a hamburger are bad enough. No picante on my eggs. But I want them hot. I don't like cold scrambled eggs."

Vivian didn't bother to respond to that. She just turned and walked away, presumably to turn in our orders.

"Does that price include the coffee?" I said to her back.

She didn't bother to answer or even to look back.

"All right," Bronte said when she was gone. "Fill me in on the details. All of them."

So I did.

Chapter 11

By the time I'd explained how I'd gotten involved with the cases and filled Sheriff Bronte in on a good bit of what I knew about the complications, our breakfasts had arrived and we'd eaten most of what we'd been served. The bacon was thin and crisp, the eggs scrambled just right. They weren't cold, either. The toast had the right amount of butter on it, and even the grits were tasty. That was even more true of the gravy, which was thick and rich. No wonder Bronte had called the number four a heart attack on a plate.

Mississippi Vivian brought us a refill for our nearly empty coffee cups and took away our breakfast plates. I fiddled with my cup while Bronte mulled over all I'd told him. When he'd thought about it for a while, he said, "Who do you think got those checks out of the mail?"

"I don't have any idea," I told him. "All I know is that they were mailed to John B.'s office. What happened to them after they got there is something I know nothing about."

I had my suspicions, of course, and he probably did as well, but I wasn't going to bring mine up, and he didn't say anything about his, either.

"What if the envelopes were tampered with before they got there?" he said.

"That's a possibility. I plan to talk to the postmaster and the mail carrier, but for right now I can't say what happened to those checks."

"You don't think Carolyn Lacy had anything to do with it, do you?"

Now we were getting down to it. I shook my head. "It's like I said. I just don't know."

"She's a fine woman."

He was the sheriff, and he knew as well as I did that being a fine woman didn't mean you wouldn't open some envelopes.

"That's what everybody tells me," I said.

"What about those injured men?"

I grinned at him.

"The ones who *allege* they were injured, then," he said. "What about them?"

"I don't know that they had anything to do with the mail problem. They might have, but that's another thing I don't know. I do know that I have to prove their allegations were false. That part of things is as simple as that. Or it would be simple if I could get any cooperation from certain people."

"What people would those be?"

"Kathy Hull is one of them. She's the only one I've talked to. I need to look at the personnel records at the tractor company to see if any of those men were working when they claimed to be injured and incapable of that sort of work. If I can prove they were, I'd have the evidence I need."

"Why the tractor place? What about the lumberyard? Didn't you say some of them were working there?"

"Sure. But I haven't had a chance to go there yet." I took a drink of my coffee. It was about the right temperature now. "I've met Kathy Hull, and she refused to let me look at the records. She said it was a matter of loyalty to her employees."

"She doesn't have to let you look at them," Bronte said. "Those records are private."

"I know she doesn't have to let me see them. It would make things easier if she would, though. I don't want to know any personal details. I just want to know who worked there and when. That kind of information's not private."

"If Kathy said she wasn't going to let you see them, you might as well forget it. She's not going to let you."

"You know her pretty well, then?"

Bronte grinned and looked me in the eye. "Kathy Hull is a hell of a woman. So is her mother."

It seemed to me that everybody I'd met wanted to impress me with what fine upstanding citizens Carolyn Lacy and her daughter were. For all I knew, it might even be true. But I wasn't entirely convinced. Even a sheriff can be wrong.

"Kathy runs that tractor shop better than any man ever did," Bronte went on. "They had two or three of them there before her, and they weren't worth a durn compared to her. I'll talk to her myself and see if that will help you get a look at those records, but I can't promise anything."

"I'd appreciate the help," I said. "I know you can't make any promises, but I don't think anybody will turn down the sheriff."

"You don't know Kathy, then," Bronte said, giving his head a little shake. "I'll give it a try, though."

I nodded and looked around the café. There was a hum of conversation, and I could hear the cook talking to Mississippi Vivian where she stood at the order window. Nobody appeared to be at all interested in what Bronte and I were discussing, but for all I knew they were straining to hear every word. For that matter, some of the very men I was interested in might be sitting at the counter or at one of the other tables and I'd never know it.

"There's one other thing I can do for you," Bronte said.

I turned my attention back to him. "What's that?"

"I can give you a statement nobody in Losgrove knew anything about those men being hurt while they were working in Houston."

"You can speak for the whole town?"

Bronte looked hurt. "I know I never heard a word, from anybody, about them being hurt. That's not good enough for you?"

"It's good enough for me, but maybe not for the company I work for. You might know all the local talk, but you might not know everything that's been discussed behind closed doors."

"I take it you don't want my statement, then."

"Not at the moment. Tell me something. What kind of medical care do you have here in Losgrove? Any doctors in town?"

I wasn't sure there would be. In fact, I doubted it. Losgrove wasn't exactly the kind of place you'd expect a general practitioner to put down roots.

"We have a little hospital," Bronte said, surprising me. "Four doctors."

My surprise must have shown in my face.

"It's a nice-sized little town," Bronte said. "We don't have a big population, but we do have a hospital. It serves the whole county, and the doctors stay plenty busy."

"I need to talk to them," I said. "They should be able to tell me if they've had any of my claimants as patients and treated them for work-related injuries."

Bronte looked doubtful. "They can't talk to you about that. They're bound by law not to talk about their patients."

Every time I came up with a way to find out something, Bronte gave me a reason why I couldn't do it. I was beginning to wonder about how much help he was going to be.

"You got a list of those claimants I could see?" he said.

I picked up my briefcase and got out the list. "Here it is." I handed it across the table. "Names and dates of the supposed injuries are all there."

He took the list from me, looked it over without comment, and handed it back to me.

"What else you got in there?" he said when I put the list back in the briefcase. "Anything I need to see?"

"I have the canceled checks," I said. "Maybe you can tell me who endorsed them."

I let him have a look at the checks. He flipped them over and looked at the endorsements, but he wasn't any help.

"Just looks like chicken scratching to me," he said. "Whoever endorsed those can't write any better than I can. No way to tell who did the writing."

Maybe that was the idea, I thought. I took the checks and put them back in the briefcase. As I did, Mississippi Vivian came over with more coffee. I put my hand over my cup, but Bronte took another refill. He liked it hot, and he took a sip almost as soon as it was poured.

I looked out the window of the café at the nearly deserted street. While we'd eaten and talked, customers had come and gone, but none had lingered. I supposed they'd gone on to their jobs if they had them, or to their homes. Just another day in small-town America.

Except that it wasn't. Something was going on here in Losgrove. I didn't know what it was, but I was determined to find out.

"Did you recognize any of the names on that list?" I said.

Bronte sat with his hands clasped around his coffee cup.

"I recognized most of them. But then I know just about everybody in the county."

"Including the men on my list?"

He was about to answer when Kathy Hull walked into the café. She looked around and saw us sitting there. She started to turn away, but I stood up and waved her over. She came, but she didn't look too happy about seeing me. Maybe it was because I was with the sheriff. Or maybe I didn't have as much natural charm as I thought I had.

Joe stood up as she approached the table and said, "Good morning, Kathy. Good to see you. Why don't you join us for breakfast?"

He was being downright courtly. I wondered if he was always like that or if it was behavior reserved for Kathy Hull.

"Thanks, Joe," she said, "but I'm waiting for my mother. We'll just sit at another table."

"I hope Carolyn's doing well."

Maybe Carolyn was the reason he was being so polite. I might have to look into their relationship before this was all over.

"My mother's fine," Kathy said, looking at me when she said it.

Bronte smiled. "Glad to hear it. You sure you won't sit down with us while you wait?"

"I'm sure."

She turned away to leave, but Joe stopped her with a touch on her arm.

"You know Ted Stephens, I think," he said.

She looked at me like she might look at a cockroach she'd seen scuttling across the café floor while she was eating.

"I've met him."

She put a lot into those few words. None of it was good.

The sheriff didn't notice, or if he did, he pretended he didn't. "He tells me he asked for a look at your personnel records at the tractor place, but you turned him down."

"That's right. Those records are none of his business. They're private."

"He just wants to know some dates of employment, nothing personal. I'd take it as a favor if you'd let him have a look at them."

Kathy smiled at me. It wasn't a nice smile. It seemed as if the air-conditioning in the café had suddenly lowered the temperature by ten degrees.

"I like you, Sheriff," she said, "and I'd help you out if I could. But I don't owe anything to Mr. Stephens. If he wants to look at those records, he's welcome to do it. If he has a court order." She gave me another one of those smiles. "Otherwise, he can forget about it."

Bronte might have said something else, but Carolyn Lacy came through the door.

"There's my mother," Kathy said. "It was nice to see you, Sheriff."

I noticed she didn't say it was nice to see me. I tried not to let my hurt feelings show.

She went to join Carolyn. They spoke briefly in low tones. Carolyn gave a quick glance in our direction, and then they found a table at the other end of the room.

"I don't think Kathy likes you very much," Bronte said.

"Hard to believe," I said. "Me being so full of charm and charisma."

"I'll talk to Carolyn," he said. "Sometimes she can get Kathy to do something when nobody else can."

He sure did know a lot about those two, I thought.

"You really believe she can get Kathy to let me see those records?" I said.

"Nope."

"That's what I thought," I said.

"Now," Bronte said, "what were we talking about?"

"My list. You were going to tell me if you knew all the men on it. But there's just one of them I'm really interested in right now."

"Which one?"

"Percy Segal."

Bronte gave me a look that made Kathy's feel like a summer day by comparison.

"You son of a bitch," he said.

Chapter 12

We got out of the café in a hurry after that. I thought for a second that Bronte might hit me, but he didn't. He didn't even touch me. He just stood up and said, "We're leaving."

I picked up my briefcase and waited for him to make a move. He just stood there. So did I.

"You first," he said.

I didn't see any need to make him tell me a second time. I tucked the briefcase under my arm and started for the door. When we were almost there, I said, "I didn't pay the check."

"It's on me," Bronte said. He turned his head and called out to Mississippi Vivian. "Put it on my tab."

She was behind the counter, but she heard him. "Sure, Joe. Ya'll come back."

I wasn't sure I'd be coming back if Bronte had his way. I figured he might take me out on some country road and do away with me. He looked angry enough.

"Get in the car," he said as soon as we were outside.

I got in and closed the door. I didn't ask where we were going. I wasn't sure I wanted to know, and anyway it didn't take long to find out. We were going to the jail.

A jail doesn't have to look like a bad place. A county can fix it up, have some flower beds around it, keep the grass trimmed, make it look like someplace you wouldn't have a bad time in. Some counties in Texas did that. Not Losgrove, Mississippi, though. The jail looked like it might have been built not long after the late unpleasantness with the Yankees, with thick stone walls and real bars on the small windows. There were no flowers, and there wasn't much grass, either. Just dirt. I wondered if the jailer's name was Torquemada.

Bronte pulled to a stop in front of the jail in a place reserved for him.

"Get out," he said.

I got out and stood beside the car.

"You first," he said.

I went up the narrow concrete walk to the steel door.

"Open it," Bronte said.

I opened it and he nudged me inside. The first thing I noticed was that the jail was air-conditioned, for which I was glad. Maybe I wouldn't sweat so much.

Bronte marched me right past the dispatcher with only a nod and herded me through another door and down a hallway. We came to a stop in front of yet another door.

"Get in there," he said.

I stood right where I was and turned to face him.

"You've been giving a lot of orders in the last few minutes. I've been following them like a good little boy, but now I'm getting tired of it. I'm not going another step further until you tell me what the hell's going on."

Bronte's face was red. I hoped he was taking his blood-pressure medication, assuming he was on it, of course.

"You want to know what's going on?" he said. "All right, I'll tell you. You're what's going on. I thought you were a reasonable man, but I can see that's not the way it is. You're just another damn' troublemaker."

He stopped. I could tell he wanted to say more, maybe something like, "and we have ways of dealing with troublemakers here in Losgrove."

He didn't say it, though, which was just as well. I'd have

laughed at him, and then he might've had to shoot me. I opened the door and looked into an interrogation room. There was nothing in there except a table and a couple of metal folding chairs. Part of the wall opposite the door was a two-way mirror.

"Go on," Bronte said, giving me another little nudge. "Get in there."

I got in there. It smelled of stale sweat, a little like a gymnasium. I walked over to the table and laid my briefcase on it, then looked at Bronte.

"What now? You bring in the goons to work me over with a rubber hose?"

"You're a real funny fella, Stephens. You know that?"

"I do have a pretty good sense of humor. You think I could get a job being a comedian like Bob Hope?"

"Comedian, my ass. I think you better sit down and shut up."

That seemed like a reasonable request, considering the circumstances, so I pulled one of the metal chairs away from the table and sat. The tabletop was scarred and covered with cigarette burns. I didn't see any ashtrays, however.

"We'll bring you in an ashtray if you want one," Bronte said in answer to my unasked question. "I notice you don't smoke, though, so not having one won't make any difference to you."

He closed the door and walked over to the table. I thought he was going to sit down, but instead he stood on the other side of the table and looked across at me. The light glinted off his glasses.

"Percy Segal," he said.

"Uncommon name, Percy," I said. "I think he preferred *Perce.*"

"I know what he preferred, dammit. Why did you want to know about him in particular."

"Well," I said, "it seems that he's dead. That kind of makes him more interesting than the other men on my little list."

"What's interesting about being dead?"

"It's not so much that he's dead that interests me," I said. "It's the way he died."

"Suicide," Bronte said. "Shot himself. Case closed."

"Self-inflicted gunshot wound."

"That's exactly right."

"Sure it is," I said. "But it sounds like a fishy case to me. I've investigated a suicide or two, and read about a lot of them. This is the only one I ever heard of where somebody went to a friend's house to kill himself."

Bronte hooked the other metal chair with his foot and pulled it away from the table. He sat down, leaned forward on the table, and said, "You sure do know a lot for a fella who just got into town."

"People like to talk to me. It's my innocent face. Didn't you think Segal's suicide was fishy?"

"Here's something maybe you don't know. Perce killed himself with Wade Dickie's shotgun."

"I heard it was a rifle."

"Well, you heard wrong."

That was possible. Mississippi Vivian might be a good waitress, but that didn't make her a firearms expert.

"Doesn't matter," I said. "Perce still went to Dickie's house to do the deed. Doesn't sound right to me."

"Maybe he didn't have a shotgun," Bronte said. "He needed a weapon, and he knew Wade had one. That's why he went to Wade's house. You can see how it was."

"How did he do it?" I said.

"How? He stuck the gun to his chest and pulled the trigger."

"Twelve gauge?"

Bronte nodded.

"Must have had the barrel cut off, then. Otherwise he'd never be able to reach the trigger. Was it cut all the way off or just part of the way? Or did he use his toe?"

Bronte leaned back in his chair, folded his arms across his chest, and looked at me. I didn't know what he expected me to do. Maybe he was trying to see if I'd blink first. I sat and looked back at him. It took a while, but he blinked.

"What the hell's your interest in how Perce Segal died?" he said.

"I'm an investigator, so just call it an investigator's curiosity. Just a natural thing, I guess. And there's the little fact that I think he's the one who got all this business started in Houston, recruited the men here, maybe set up the whole deal. You can see why I might be a little curious about his death, seeing as I won't be able to talk to him."

Bronte opened his mouth, and I thought he might be about to tell me something, but before he could say anything there was a knock on the door.

Bronte stood up. "You just sit right there," he said, then went to the door and opened it.

I sat where I was, but I turned to see who was at the door. A uniformed deputy stood there. He asked Bronte if everything was all right.

"Everything's fine, Sherm. I'll call you if I need you."

Sherm was a big man, almost as big as I am, and a lot younger. I hoped Bronte wouldn't have to call him.

Bronte closed the door and came back to the table.

"That's a relief," I said as he sat back down.

"What's a relief?"

"Knowing that the microphone's turned off. That means nobody's recording us."

Bronte grinned. "This room's not miked. We got another one for that. We have our more private conversations in here."

"Since it's so nice and private," I said, "you can go ahead and tell me the truth. Perce Segal didn't really kill himself, did he."

"He sure as hell did. That's why I brought you here, Stephens. I wanted to make sure you believed that Perce Segal shot himself."

"You're not doing such a good job of convincing me," I told him.

"All right, then, maybe I'm not. So I'm going to go about convincing you of something else. And you know why?"

"I don't know a damn' thing," I said. "I'm just trying to find out."

"I'll tell you why, then. Buster Kerns told me that you were a good investigator, maybe the best he's ever known. He must've known plenty, being a sheriff of a big county like his."

I didn't see any reason for false modesty. "Buster knows what he's talking about."

"I figured as much. So here's what I'm going to convince you of. I'm going to convince you not to investigate Percy Segal's suicide. It's none of your business, it doesn't have anything to do with your case, and it's going to irritate the hell out of me if you do it. So don't."

He might have been telling the truth about the death having nothing to do with my investigation, but I wasn't convinced. I decided not to let him know that, however.

"I'll have to take your word for it that Segal's death has nothing to do with my investigation," I said.

"Damn' right you will. I'm going to help you all I can with your other cases, but not that one. That's nothing to do with you. Are we square on that?"

"We're square," I lied.

Maybe what he said was true, but so was what I'd told him about my natural curiosity. There wasn't anything I could do about it. I'd poke around, but I'd keep it from Bronte.

"If you go nosing around where you shouldn't, you'll be in a mess," Bronte said, as if he'd read my mind. "Traffic tickets every time you turn around, tickets for littering. Little aggravations like that. Won't hurt you much, but they'll slow you down, take up your time. You wouldn't want that, would you?"

"No," I said. "I wouldn't want that."

"Good. Then I guess we understand each other."

"Yeah," I said. "I guess we do." Not that I was going to go along with what he wanted, even if I did understand it. "Now can I go? Unless you want to pistol-whip me just to be sure I have everything straight."

"You can go. You can do all the investigating you want to about those claims of yours. I'll even help you if I can. But Perce Segal's suicide is off limits."

"I'm not interested in that."

I stood up, wondering if he believed me. It would make things easier if he did, but I didn't care one way or the other. I was going to follow the investigation wherever it led me, and, if it led me to Segal's death, I wasn't going to back off. That's just the way I am. I had a feeling Bronte suspected as much, but he didn't let it show.

"I'll take you back to the motel," he said.

"That's all right. I'll walk. It's not far, and I can use the fresh air."

He looked insulted, but he didn't say anything. I went to the door. It wasn't locked, so I went out and down the hall. The dispatcher paid me no attention, and then I was outside and breathing the humid fresh air of Losgrove.

Chapter 13

The more I thought about what Bronte had said and the way he said it, the less I liked it. So instead of going back to the motel, I walked back to the Magnolia Café. Mississippi Vivian met me at the door.

"Do you ever go home?" I asked her.

"Now and then. What can I get for you."

The walk from the jail had made me uncomfortably warm. My shirt was sticking to my back. The air-conditioning helped, but a cold drink would help even more.

"How about a Dr Pepper? Ice cold if you have it."

"We have it," she said.

She went to get the drink, and I went to what I was beginning to think of as my usual table. There were only a couple of other people in the café, and no one was sitting nearby.

When Vivian brought the drink in a tall glass with ice and a straw, I asked her if she had time to sit down for a few minutes. She glanced around at the customers and saw that her services wouldn't be required for a while.

"I guess so. Are we going to have another talk?"

"Sort of." I sipped some Dr Pepper through the straw. The liquid was so cold that I could feel it as it went down through my esophagus. Just what I needed. "Where does Wade Dickie live?"

"Why do you want to know?"

Well, okay, I admit it. I should have known that was coming.

I'd practically asked for it.

"I'd like to talk to him," I said.

"What about?"

Mississippi Vivian, in her own little way, was one of the most aggravating people I'd ever run across. And I included myself in that group.

"About Percy Segal. And his suicide."

"You can't talk to him at home."

"And why is that?"

"I thought you were a big-time private eye, like Peter Gunn."

"Peter Gunn?" I said.

"On TV. He was a big-time private eye."

It took me a second or two, but I remembered. I'd never seen the show, but I'd heard of it.

"That was a long time ago," I said.

"What difference does that make?"

She had a point. "None. Why did you mention him in the first place?"

"Because you ought to remember that I told you where Wade was when Percy shot himself."

I remembered that, too, now that she'd brought it up.

"At work," I said. "At the lumberyard. And his wife works at the drugstore."

"I knew you could figure it out if you tried. Peter Gunn always did that. That was a good-looking man who played him on TV. I can't remember his name."

I wasn't interested in his name. I thanked Vivian for her time and drank a little more Dr Pepper.

"Where's the lumberyard?" I said.

"You going to talk to Wade?"

"I just want to find the lumberyard. If Wade's there, I might talk to him. But I can't talk to him if I can't get to where he is. Maybe I could buy a map of the town."

"You don't have to do that. I can tell you where the lumberyard is."

"I know you can," I said. "But will you?"

"Two blocks over to your right when you go out the door and then three blocks to your left."

I thanked her for giving me a straight answer at last and finished my drink.

"Put it on the sheriff's tab," I said as I got up to leave.

Mississippi Vivian laughed. "I'll do it. But if I get arrested, you'll have to go my bail."

"You can count on me," I told her.

I stepped outside into the heat and regretted that I hadn't let Bronte take me to the motel for my car. Now I was going to have to walk to the lumberyard or go to the motel on foot. I decided that I might as well go on to the lumberyard as to walk back for the car. I was glad my leg wasn't bothering me.

I walked the two blocks to the south, stopping to look in through the window of John B.'s office as I passed by. Carolyn sat at the desk, but she didn't see me. I kept on walking. I passed a little auto-parts store, a dry cleaner's, and a drugstore. After I turned left, I went by an insurance office, a clothing store, a jewelry store, and another lawyer's office. I wondered who in Losgrove bought enough jewelry to keep a jewelry store in business.

The lumberyard took up a whole block all on its own. It was more modern than I'd expected, with what I figured was a newly remodeled building with a big sign out front. It was actually as much a hardware store as a lumberyard, though I could see the lumber sheds in the back.

I went in through the front door. The big rectangular room was well-lit with rows of fluorescent bulbs above long racks filled with a lot of things that had very little to do with lumber:

batteries, light bulbs, plumbing supplies, electrical wire, and other kinds of hardware. In the middle of the room there was a three-sided counter with cash registers on two sides. There was only one cashier, however, and he wasn't doing any business. He seemed happy to see me come in.

"What can I do for you?" he said by the time I'd taken two steps inside.

He was a big, gap-toothed redhead with freckles and a wide country grin, and I hated to tell him that I wasn't a potential customer.

"I'm looking for the bookkeeper," I said. "I need to talk to her about a business matter."

I didn't say whose business; it wasn't any of his.

"She's in the office."

He pointed to his left, where there was a cubicle with a window in the side. I saw a middle-aged woman sitting at a desk, pecking away at an old manual typewriter. I wondered what she could be writing. Business letters, maybe.

I thanked the clerk, who'd already lost interest in me, and walked over to the cubicle. It had no ceiling, but it did have a door with a window set in the top half. I tapped on the glass, and the woman looked away from the typewriter and at me. She nodded, and I opened the door and went inside.

"Yes?" she said. "Can I help you?"

I introduced myself. She told me she was Gail Cole and invited me to have a seat. I sat in a metal chair with a plastic bottom and told her that I was in Losgrove as part of an investigation for an insurance company.

"Well, Mr. Stephens," she said, "that's all very interesting, I'm sure, but I don't see what it has to do with me."

She had a soft voice and that Mississippi accent that everyone in town shared. I was beginning to like it. I liked the smile lines at the corners of her mouth, too.

"Please call me Ted," I said. "And I'll tell you what my investigation has to do with you."

"All right, Ted. That sounds interesting. I'd like to hear what you have to say."

I patted the briefcase that lay on my lap. "To tell you the truth, Gail, this doesn't really have a thing to do with you. But it does have to do with some of your employees."

"Oh," she said. "I'll bet you mean the Houston boys."

"The Houston boys?" I said. "Who are they?"

"They're a bunch of men that went off to work in Houston for a while. They must not have liked it there because they all came back here after a while. Not a very long while, either. Some people don't like the big cities, you know. It's a lot quieter in a place like Losgrove, but it's home, and the people who've lived here for a long time like it a lot."

"So those 'Houston boys' have been around Losgrove for a while?"

"Their whole lives, most of them. It's no wonder they didn't like it in the city." She smiled. "Not that I mean any offense by that. I'm sure Houston must have a lot of things to recommend it, but they're small-town folks."

I shrugged. "Houston's a city. Terrible traffic, chemical plants and refineries putting stuff in the air, and lord knows what's in the water of the Ship Channel. But I still like the city."

"Well, those boys from here didn't. They're not really boys. I shouldn't call them that. They're all grown men, but some of us have known them most of their lives."

"Maybe they didn't like Houston because they all got injured on the job while they were there," I said.

She smiled again. "I have to be honest with you, Mr. Stephens. Ted. I know a little more about why you're here than I let on."

I'd already figured that out for myself. "Seems like most

people in town know more than they let on."

"That's the way it is here. It's hard to keep a secret around here."

It wasn't as hard as she was making it out to be. The secret of Percy Segal's death was pretty well kept if you asked me. And I was sure there was a secret.

This wasn't the time to bring that topic up, however. I wanted another kind of information from her, the kind that Kathy Hull wouldn't give me, for some reason or other, and I'd have to get that first. If I did, maybe I could get her to talk about Segal.

"Since it's so hard to keep a secret in this town, you probably know why I'm here talking to you," I said.

"I have a pretty good idea. Those men we call the Houston boys must be involved in those claims you're looking into."

"You got it right with your first try," I told her. "It's my job to find out if they're telling the truth."

"They never mentioned being hurt on the job while they were in Houston," she said. "I guess that doesn't mean much, though."

"I'd be more than happy to take your word for that, but it doesn't prove a thing. They could just be toughing it out."

"Some of them are pretty tough, all right. That's not much help, either, is it."

"No, but you could help me out quite a bit if you would."

"How?" she said.

I thought she knew. She just wanted me to ask her. Some people are like that. They think that if you have to ask, you'll owe them a favor later on if they ever need one. I'm always glad to provide a little *quid pro quo,* if I feel like it. So far she hadn't given me any reason to feel obligated.

"Well," I said, "to start with, you could tell me if any of the Houston boys had any injuries before they went to Houston. I mean serious injuries that would keep them from doing any work."

"You mean, if somebody dumped a load of shingles on them?" She smiled to show she was just joking.

"That would do it, all right," I said. "Did any of them ever file any claims on the lumberyard?"

"Not a one of them, and none of them ever got hurt here. We have a very good safety record."

So none of the men had been hurt before taking the jobs on the docks. I'd thought maybe some of them could have been using an old injury and claiming that it was a new one. Obviously that wasn't the case.

"I'd like to look at your personnel records," I said. "Not to see anything that I'm not supposed to see. All I want to know is whether any of those men took off work to visit a doctor any time within the last six months."

"I can tell you that without looking at the records. Those boys never take any time off. Some of them even get a little overtime. They're all good workers."

"Not that I don't believe you," I said, "but it would help if I could verify that. It would help even more if I could make copies of their records for my boss. Do you think that would be all right?"

"I don't see why not," she said. "You won't have to make copies, though. I'm sure I have carbons of everything, and I could let you have those. We don't really need them since we have the originals."

"That would be even better," I said.

She smiled. "Let me check the files."

She walked over to a gun-metal-gray filing cabinet and opened one of the drawers. She flipped through the folders with the familiarity of long practice. She obviously knew what she was doing, and I admired her ability to do it. I've never had much talent for filing things away and keeping them in their proper places. It's one of my many failings. I have people I can call on when I need information, and they can find it for me fast. I've come to rely on them, maybe a little too much. It wasn't that way when I'd started out in the business, and now and then I sort of miss the days when I actually had to dig to get the information for myself. Not often, though.

It took only a couple of minutes. Gail located the carbons and handed them over to me. I glanced at them and saw that everything I needed was there. I was interested in one name in particular. Percy Segal. I laid one of the sheets on the desk and put my finger on Segal's name, careful not to smear the carbon.

"I believe this man's dead," I said.

Gail's eyes narrowed, and her smile lines disappeared.

"That son of a bitch," she said.

Chapter 14

Bronte had called me a son of a bitch when I brought up Segal's death, and now here was Gail Cole using the same phrase. She wasn't talking about me, which I appreciated.

"My grandmother told me never to speak ill of the dead," I said.

"Your grandmother never had a man shoot himself in her best friend's house, then," Gail said.

I took the paper off the desk, put it with the others, and stuck them all in my briefcase. It was a good thing I had them already because I don't think Gail liked me anymore. Though she probably liked me more than she did Percy Segal.

"I'm sure that was inconvenient for Mrs. Dickie," I said.

"You don't know the half of it."

"And for Perce Segal, too."

"I don't want to talk about him."

"I'm just curious. What would cause a man to kill himself at another person's house?"

Gail's face had hardened. No smile lines to be seen. She might never have smiled in her life for all her face showed.

"He was crazy, that's why." She stood up. "I've given you what you came for. Now I think it's time for you to leave."

I can take a hint. I thanked her for helping me out, and I left. I had a feeling that Gail disliked Percy for more than the fact that he'd killed himself at her friend's house. Maybe she was one of the women he'd been fooling around with. But I wasn't satisfied with that answer. I wanted to know more about Percy Segal's death. Fortunately there were at least two more people I could talk to about it, so I stopped at the checkout counter and asked the freckled young man if he knew where I could find Wade Dickie.

"He's out back loading a truck."

"Thanks," I said.

"You going to talk to him?" he said as I started away from the counter. "The boss doesn't like it when people don't do their jobs."

He hadn't said anything when I wanted to talk to the bookkeeper. Maybe he didn't think her work was important. I looked around the place. I hadn't seen anybody who seemed to be in charge of things, so I said, "Where's the boss?"

"He's not here right now."

"I guess you're in charge, then."

He gave me his big grin. "I guess I am."

"Well, I won't keep Mr. Dickie from doing his job. He can talk and work at the same time."

"All right, but he better not sit down. It's not his break time."

"I'll see to it that he doesn't," I said and headed out the back door.

When I went through the door, I found myself standing on a concrete loading dock. There was nobody else around. I could smell the good scent of freshly cut wood. The lumber sheds looked like those of any other lumberyard, long racks of lumber covered by metal roofs. Down at the end of the gravel row in front of the dock, a couple of men were loading bags on the flat bed of a black lumber truck.

I walked down the steps at the end of the dock and went down to where the men were working. As I got closer, I could see that the bags held concrete mix. I've handled bags like that once or twice, and they're hard to work with, packed solid, slick, not easy to get hold of. But the men seemed to be having an easy enough time of it. I recognized the one under the shed. He was Johnny Turner. He picked up the bags and handed them across to the man standing on the truck bed. That one took them, swung around, and stacked them in neat, solid rows.

I stood and watched them for a minute. It was hot work, and their tan shirts were soaked through with sweat that turned them dark, almost black, under the arms and on the backs, but they didn't seem bothered by that. They had a steady rhythm going, and they'd have the truck loaded before long.

They kept right on loading for a couple of minutes, not paying any attention to me. Then Johnny Turner noticed me. He stopped what he was doing and gave me a hard look. He didn't like me any more today than he had yesterday.

"What are you doing here?" he said.

"I'm looking for Wade Dickie," I told him. "I was told he was working out here."

The man on the truck bed gave me the once-over. "I'm Wade Dickie. What do you want with me?"

He was a middle-aged man, big through the shoulders, and obviously strong. Otherwise he couldn't have been handling those heavy sacks as easily as he did. If he'd been hurt on the docks in Houston, he'd made a miraculous recovery.

"I want to talk to you about Percy Segal."

Percy's name hadn't gotten a good reaction from anybody I'd talked to that day, and Wade was no exception.

"Too bad," he said. "I don't talk about that son of a bitch."

It was nice to know that everybody had the same high opinion of old Perce.

Wade looked at Turner, who picked up a bag and handed it to Dickie. Dickie caught it smoothly and put it in the stack he'd been working on.

"You're the one I need to talk to," I told Wade. "It was your house he killed himself in."

Wade turned back to me and brushed the sweat off his forehead with one hand. He wiped his hand on the front of his shirt and said, "I know where he killed himself. He should've done it somewhere else if he had to do it, but he picked my place. I can't help what he did. He's dead, and that's that."

"I think there's more to it than that."

Wade grinned. "Guess what?"

I told him I wasn't a good guesser.

"I'll tell you then. I don't give a damn what you think!"

I said I wasn't surprised. "But I'm just trying to do a job, just like you are."

He looked me over. He didn't seem thrilled with what he saw.

"Not like I am," he said. "What do you think, Johnny?"

Johnny grinned. "I don't think he ever got his hands dirty in his life."

I could've said *not since I touched you with one of them,* but I was much too polite. Besides, it wouldn't have made any difference. Turner and Dickie had already decided they didn't like me in the least.

Turner picked up another bag of concrete mix. Dickie gave him the slightest of nods. Maybe they thought I wouldn't see it, or maybe they thought I wouldn't catch on. Maybe they even thought I was too old and slow to do anything even if I knew what was coming.

They were wrong about the first two. They might have been close on that third one, but I still managed to dodge to the side before the bag that Turner tossed my way could hit me. It landed on the gravel and split open. Gray dust billowed up and almost made me sneeze.

"Now look what you've made Johnny do," Dickie said. I could tell he was disappointed that the bag hadn't hit me. "You'll have to pay for that."

"Let 'em dock Johnny's pay," I said.

Dickie didn't reply to that. Instead he jumped down from the bed of the truck, landing about six feet from me. I didn't have any doubts about his intent. He was going to beat the crap out of me.

My briefcase was tucked under my arm. I pulled it out and poked it in Dickie's direction. As was only natural, he paused and looked at it. I dropped it. He wouldn't have been human if he hadn't looked at it when it fell.

That was a mistake, of course, as he was about to find out. The hard way.

In the second his eyes were off me, I covered the distance between us, and, when he looked down, I clubbed him in the side of the neck right behind his ear. The next thing he knew, he was on his knees in the gravel, head down, still looking at the briefcase but not seeing it, I figured.

I wasn't planning to hit him again, which was a good thing because Johnny Turner had finally figured out what was going on. He jumped to the ground and started a mighty swing from somewhere around Arkansas. I guess he thought he was going to flatten me with a single punch. I don't know where these youngsters learn to fight. I could have taught him a thing or two, but there was no use in putting myself at a disadvantage. I stepped inside the telegraphed punch and slammed him in the left eye with the heel of my right hand. I was afraid that I might have damaged his eyesight, but then I decided I didn't really care.

Dickie shook his head and tried to move. He was game. I had to give him that. He came about halfway up off his knees and made a dive for me. I made a little sidestep, and kicked him in the ribs.

I was careful to kick him with my left leg. If I'd kicked him with the right, the old war wound wouldn't have liked it. Even with the left leg, though, I was pretty good. The kick lifted him up six inches or so higher than he'd been, and then he fell flat on his face. The gravel probably wasn't going to do it any good.

Nearby, Turner sat on his butt with his hands on his face, blubbering and whining that I'd blinded him.

I picked up my briefcase and dusted it off.

"You'll be fine," I told him. "If I'd wanted to blind you, your eyeballs would be on the ground somewhere, and you'd be feeling around for them with both hands. You'll have a pretty good shiner, though. Better not tell the girls that some old man beat you up. Tell 'em it was a motorcycle gang or something."

He said something that was probably uncomplimentary, but I ignored it because he was mumbling and I couldn't understand any of it.

Dickie was trying to sit up, so I helped him a little and then dragged him over by the lumber truck and propped him up in the shade where it was a little cooler. That was me, a kindly old gentleman, helping people in need wherever he could.

It had become obvious that Dickie wasn't going to talk to me, much less tell me anything useful, and Turner didn't like me a whole lot, either. So it was time for me to leave.

Which is exactly what I would've done if something hadn't prevented it. At the end of the row, the sheriff's car slid to a stop, skidding a little on the gravel.

It was a long way back to the other end of the row, but it wouldn't have done me any good to go that way, as another county car turned the corner and headed in my direction. I might have been able to get back to the loading dock and go out through the front door, but it was hot, and I'd already worked up a sweat. I didn't see any use in running and getting even hotter. So I stood where I was and waited.

Joe Bronte got out of the car nearest me, putting on his straw hat as he walked in my direction. The deputy's car stopped about ten yards from me, and the deputy opened the door. I expected him to stand there behind it and throw down on me from the classic two-handed pose, but he didn't. He closed the door and stood there, one hand on his pistol butt and the other fiddling with his baton.

He was a compact young black man who looked as if he might have been a pretty good minor-league shortstop or maybe a second baseman who'd stopped one too many hard grounders with his nose, which was a little flat and off-kilter. His uniform shirt was dark brown and crisp as were his khaki pants. He wasn't wearing a hat, and his brush-cut hair was almost the same color as his shirt. I wondered how many black men were deputy sheriffs in Mississippi. The times, as Bob Dylan said, were a-changin'. Dylan wasn't much of a singer in my book, not like Jim Croce, say, but now and then he made a good point.

"Got a call about somebody here disturbing the peace," Bronte said. "Would that have been you, Ted?"

"Not me," I said. "I haven't made a single call today."

Bronte didn't laugh. I really was going to have to work on my delivery. He said, "I meant was it you who was disturbing the peace."

I wondered who'd made the call. Either Gail Cole or the kid who was in charge. I'd have put my money on Gail.

"I haven't been disturbing anybody," I said. "I'm just a good Samaritan, helping out the less fortunate who've fallen off a lumber truck."

Bronte looked over at Dickie, who was still propped against the wheel of the truck. Then he glanced toward Turner, who had moved over in the shade as well. He still had his hand over his face.

"Turner bumped into a two-by-four that was sticking out of the end of a stack," I said. "Dickie was going to help him, and they both fell off the back of the truck. I was just seeing what I could do to make them more comfortable."

Bronte nodded. "Uh-huh. You believe that, Ellis?"

"Uh-huh," the deputy said. "But then I believe in Santy Claus and the Tooth Fairy."

"But not the Easter Bunny?" I said.

The deputy grinned at me. "Him, too. Or her. I could never tell much about the sex of a rabbit."

"They have a lot of it, or so I hear."

He laughed, and I thought maybe I could get him into a discussion about rabbits, but Bronte had other ideas. He went over to Dickie and gave him a nudge with the toe of his rubber-soled shoe.

"Hey, Wade," he said.

Dickie looked up at him. Dickie's face wasn't too bad, I thought. A good wash with soap and water, and you'd hardly know he'd hit the gravel with it, except for maybe a couple of places where the skin was broken.

"You all right?" Bronte said.

"Yeah. I fell off the truck, landed pretty hard. But I'm okay."

"Uh-huh," Bronte said. "What about you, Turner?"

"I think I blinded myself in one eye," Turner said.

Bronte went over to him. "Let me take a look."

Turner took his hands away from his face and gave Bronte a look at his eye.

"Can you see me?" Bronte said.

"Yeah, I can see you."

"Close your good eye."

Turner closed it. That made him squinch up his left eye. I could see that the skin around it was already starting to darken. He was going to have quite a bruise all right. Maybe that would teach him not to pick on defenseless old men.

"How many fingers am I holding up?" Bronte said, holding up three.

"Three. They're a little blurry, but I can see 'em."

Bronte dropped his hand. "You'll be fine, then. Get up, go get yourself a drink of water, and then get back to work. Mr. Lawson won't like it if he catches you loafing on the job. Same for you, Wade. That is, if you can get up."

"I can get up," Wade said.

He used the wheel of the truck and then grabbled hold of the bed to help himself out, but he got up all right.

"I might need a hand," Turner said. "I'm a little shaky."

"Help him out, Wade," Bronte said.

Dickie walked over a little unsteadily and put out a hand. Turner took hold, and Dickie pulled. I thought for a second Turner might get about halfway up and then drag Dickie on top of him, but it didn't happen. They stood side by side for a second, then waddled off in search of the water fountain.

"Fell off the truck, huh?" Bronte said to me.

"Yeah," I said. "It was a hell of a thing. I'm just glad I was here to help out."

"I'll bet you are." Bronte looked over my shoulder. "You can get on back to patrol now, Ellis. I think I can handle this all by myself from here on out."

Ellis didn't say anything. I heard the door slam and the car start. Then there was some backing and filling before gravel spurted from under the tires.

"You didn't do anything to cause Wade to fall, I guess," Bronte said.

"Not me. I was just out here looking things over."

"According to Miz Cole, you were asking her about Perce Segal. I believe I told you not to go doing that."

His voice was level and low, but I could tell he was a little bit steamed at me. It was pretty plain that he hadn't believed a word of that stuff I'd fed him about Dickie and Turner, even if they'd backed me up on it, but he wasn't going to come right out and say so.

"I came here to get some information about the lumberyard's employees," I said. "That's all. Ms. Cole gave it to me." I patted the briefcase. "It's all right here."

"And you didn't bring up Perce Segal?"

"Well, I might have mentioned his name. You didn't tell me not to do that. You told me not to go sticking my nose where it didn't belong, or something along that line. I was just asking about Perce out of curiosity. After all, he killed himself in the house of Ms. Cole's best friend."

"Uh-huh. And then you came out here to check out the four-by-sixes."

"Right. That's exactly what I did. Always been fascinated by lumber."

I hoped he wouldn't question the kid inside and ask him if I'd said anything about looking for Wade Dickie.

"And naturally you didn't mention Perce to Wade, since you were too busy being a ministering angel."

"Right again. No wonder they keep electing you sheriff."

He gave me the fish-eye. "You're not near as funny as you think you are, Stephens."

"I know it. People tell me that all the time. I think it's my delivery. I've been working on it, trying to improve."

"It's not your delivery," Bronte said. "It's your attitude. That could use some work, too."

"I'll take that into consideration," I said.

"Sure you will. I'll tell you what, Stephens, I'm going to lay this out for you as plain as I can, and I want you to listen carefully. Can you do that?"

"I've always been a good listener," I said. "Better at that than telling jokes, anyway."

"All right, then. Here it is. I don't want you sticking your nose in where it doesn't belong."

I started to interrupt and tell him he'd said that already, but he held up his hand.

"*And* I don't want you to be asking any more questions about Perce Segal. He killed himself and that's that. Case closed. You get it?"

"I get it," I said, and I did.

That didn't mean I was going to stop asking questions, though. Mississippi Vivian had told me that there weren't any secrets in Losgrove, but she'd been wrong. There was some kind of secret relating to Perce Segal's death. I didn't know if it had anything to do with my case, but it might. So I had to find out what the secret was. That's just the kind of guy I am.

Mississippi Vivian hadn't been the only one who was wrong. I'd thought I could work with a man like Joe Bronte, but it was beginning to look as if that wasn't so. I liked him, and I believed he was an honest man, but he was trying to cover up something. I didn't like that.

"Does this mean you're not going to run me in for littering?" I said.

"Not this time. I've giving you another chance. A big-city fella doesn't know what it's like in a place like Losgrove, so he's likely to make a mistake or two. That's all he's allowed, though. After that, things can get a little rough on him."

We both knew he wasn't talking about some big-city fella in general. He was talking about one who was standing a yard or so away from him, the one named Ted Stephens.

"There come Wade and Johnny," Bronte said.

I turned and looked. Sure enough, they were on their way back to the truck.

"They're gonna get back to work," Bronte said, "and so am I. You'd better do the same, as long as your work doesn't have anything to do with Perce's suicide."

"I guess it doesn't," I said.

"Good."

Bronte got in his car and drove away. Turner and Dickie climbed back up on the truck and started to stack the sacks again without a word to me. I couldn't think of anything to say to them, either, so I walked down to the end of the row and away from there.

CHAPTER 15

I walked back to the Magnolia Café to see if my informant was there. Sure enough, Mississippi Vivian was serving up food to the lunch crowd.

I found a booth near the back and sat down. After a minute or so, Vivian was standing by the table.

"What's for lunch?" I said.

"You know what's for lunch."

"Only if it's the same thing as yesterday."

"It's not the same thing as yesterday. We don't serve leftovers here."

She knew that wasn't what I'd meant, but there was no use in arguing with her. I told her I'd have the meatloaf.

"And after I eat," I added, "we need to have a talk."

"I don't get a break for a while."

"That's all right. I can wait."

In fact, I didn't mind waiting. I ate the meatloaf, which was just as good as yesterday's, and I drank several large glasses of iced tea. When I'd done that, I opened up my briefcase and went over the records that Gail Cole had given me. As she'd said, none of the men on my list had taken any time off to see a doctor or anything else. It was all there in black and white, and it made the story that they all had severe back injuries look even flimsier than before, not that it had ever been rock solid.

After a while the crowd thinned out and Vivian came back to sit across from me in the booth.

"What do we have to talk about?" she said.

"What do you want to talk about?" I said.

She stared at me. Some people can dish it out, but they can't take it.

"Perce Segal," I said. "There's something funny about his death."

"You think a man killing himself is funny? You Houston folks sure are different."

"I didn't mean funny ha-ha. I meant funny strange. Nobody wants to talk to me about it, and Joe Bronte even warned me not to ask any questions about it."

"So here you are, asking questions. You think that's a smart thing to do?"

"I don't believe you'd say anything to him about what we say to each other. After all, we have a financial relationship."

Vivian smiled and looked at me over the tops of her glasses. "Not much of one."

I knew what she was getting at. I said, "I'm authorized to pay you another hundred dollars if you have any more information for me."

She thought that over for a while, then shook her head. "I wish I did. But I've already told you all I know. The sheriff said it was a suicide, and that's all there is to that. He's the law."

"What about the coroner?"

"He said the same thing."

I could see I wasn't going to find out anything else about Perce Segal from her. If there was a secret, and I was sure there was, it was being well kept.

"What about Johnny Turner?" I said.

"What about him?"

I suppressed a sigh. "He doesn't like me," I said.

"I hate to tell you this, but you're not the most likeable man I've ever met. Maybe you rub him the wrong way."

"And here I thought I exuded kind of a natural charm."

Vivian didn't so much as smile. It was becoming clear to me that I'm not as funny as I think I am. Moving right along, I told her about the episodes at the tractor place and the lumberyard.

"You rub him the wrong way, all right, but, come to think of it, he did have something to do with Perce in a roundabout way."

Sometimes if you just keep asking questions, you might finally come up with the information that helps you figure things out. Maybe this was it.

"What did he have to do with him?" I said.

"What about that hundred dollars?"

I took a quick glance around. Only a couple of people were still eating, and they weren't interested in us at all. I leaned to the left, pulled my billfold from my hip pocket, and took out a hundred-dollar bill. I handed the money to Vivian, and it disappeared into the pocket of her apron. There was a coffee stain on the pocket that hadn't been there earlier. Vivian was getting careless.

It wasn't the coffee stain I wanted to know about, however.

"Johnny Turner," I said.

"Well, it wasn't exactly Perce that Johnny had anything to do with," she said, and I was afraid she'd just rooked me out of a hundred dollars. "I said it was in a roundabout way, remember."

How could I forget? With her, everything was a roundabout way. I said, "Just tell me about it."

"I don't know how well Johnny knew Perce. Everybody here pretty much knows everybody else, so he must've known him a little bit. Johnny did know the Dickies, though."

"I know that. I told you that I just saw him and Wade Dickie loading concrete mix at the lumberyard. I don't think Wade likes me, either."

"You're not making a lot of friends around here, are you."

"Never mind that. Let's get back to Johnny Turner."

"He works at the lumberyard part-time."

"I know that. It's not his employment that interests me. It's his connection to Perce Segal. That's what I just paid you a hundred dollars to find out about, not where he works or that he knows Wade Dickie."

"You don't have to get snippy about it."

I didn't think I'd been snippy, but she could have been right. I moderated my tone and said, "Did Johnny Turner have anything to do with Perce or not?"

"That's what I've been trying to tell you."

She could have fooled me, but I told her to go ahead. I might as well let her tell it her way, because I sure wasn't going to get it any other way.

"You want to hear it or not?" she said.

"I want to hear it."

"All right, then. Perce was Wade Dickie's friend. Used to hang around with him."

"Shot himself at his house, too. You can't be a better friend than that."

She shook her head. "You shouldn't joke about things like that."

At least she'd recognized it as a joke, even if she didn't like it. Maybe I was getting better.

"Besides, it's not funny," she said. "Not one bit."

So I wasn't getting any better, after all. I tried to get her back on track.

"What does Perce being Dickie's friend have to do with Johnny Turner?"

"That's what I was trying to tell you before you interrupted me. Johnny works with Wade at the lumberyard."

I sighed.

"But that's not all," Vivian continued, ignoring me. "Johnny used to date Wade's daughter. Barbara."

At last, some new information. "You mentioned her," I said. "I haven't met her yet."

"You might not meet her, either. She doesn't live at home all the time, and I don't think she's living there now."

I remembered that Vivian had said something about Barbara's living elsewhere. Now I wondered why.

"Didn't get along with her father's what I heard," Vivian said. "I told you she had a reputation for being a little wild. You could ask Johnny Turner about that if you wanted to."

I didn't think Turner would be in the mood to answer any questions for me, but I might have to ask him. He was a short-tempered youngster, and I wondered what he might do if he got the idea that someone, say some older man like Percy Segal, was putting the make on his sweetie. Of course I didn't know that Perce had done anything of the kind, but it was something to think about, and there was something in Vivian's tone that indicated I was the one who should do the thinking.

I thanked Vivian for the information and told her I hadn't gotten the full hundred dollars' worth from her yet.

"That means you'll be back," she said.

"You can count on it. But not just to talk to you. I like the food here."

"I'll bet," she said.

I went back to the motel to rest up. I figured I deserved a nap after my strenuous day's work. I'm not as young as I once was, and a little nap never hurt anybody. Besides, roughing up a couple of guys isn't as easy as it used to be.

But, before I got my rest, I wanted to call Don Cogsdill and let him know how the investigation was going. He was interested in the fact that Wade Dickie didn't seem to be an invalid. He was interested in the fight, too.

"I didn't send you down there to get your tail whipped," he said.

"You must not have been listening," I said. "I was the one handing out the whippings."

"Yeah, at least in your version. And what's all this business about Percy Segal's suicide?"

"I think it ties in with the case in some way or the other. I'm not sure how, but people sure don't want me looking into it. That means there's something to hide."

"Not necessarily, and I'm not paying you to look into a suicide. Segal didn't have a life-insurance policy with our agency, so we don't owe any money for that. And we don't have the money to waste on long-distance calls talking about it. It's not our problem, or yours. It's the disability claims that we're interested in, or have you forgotten that?"

I told him I hadn't forgotten. "But like I said, the suicide might tie in. It's a pretty big coincidence that the person we think set up the whole scam has killed himself, don't you think?"

"I don't get paid to think. That's your job, and you're thinking the wrong things this time. Which reminds me. You still haven't found out about those checks. Can't you at least find out who cashed them?"

"I still need the personnel records from the tractor place," I said. "I figure we'll need a court order to get them, too. Miss Hull has made it clear that she has no intention of cooperating with me. There's something going on with her, too, and with her mother, but I don't know what it is yet."

"You don't know a hell of a lot, do you."

Don was all right, but he got impatient sometimes. He wanted results instantly, if not somewhat sooner.

"I haven't been here that long," I reminded him. "And while nearly everybody except Kathy Hull seems to want to help, I'm not getting anywhere. It's going to take some time."

"Maybe if you stopped chasing rabbits down side paths, you'd accomplish more."

"Look," I said, feeling a little exasperated, "you hired me to do a job, and you know that I have my way of doing things. Either you let me work this case my way, or you can fire me and send somebody else. It's your choice, and I don't care one way or the other."

There was silence for a second or two and then Don said, "You don't have to get pissed off at me."

"I'm not pissed off. I just want to be able to do the job the way I want to do it."

"All right. Fine. Do it your way. It wouldn't matter if I told you not to, and even if you promised to do it my way, you'd do whatever you damn well pleased."

"You know me too well," I said.

"Yeah, I do. Listen, why don't you get a confession from one of those men at the lumberyard? You're good at that kind of thing. Just get one of them to confess and name a few names. That way you can get the others to talk."

That's the trouble with being good at something like getting confessions. People think that all you have to do is put on a little pressure and people will spill everything they know to you. It's true that I'd been lucky in the past, lucky or damned good, or both. But that was no help in this case.

"All those men know they filed false claims," Don continued. "They've probably talked to each other about it. Hell, you *know* they'd talked to each other about it. Get one to admit what they did, and they'll all have to confess."

"Hearsay," I said, knowing it wouldn't do any good.

Don laughed. "Don't give me that *hearsay* crap. I know better, and so do you. It's not hearsay if all of them, or even if just some of them, got together and conspired to file false claims."

I had to agree with him on that one, so I admitted that he

was right. I might as well be big about it.

"Damn straight, I'm right," he said. "That's the way to handle it. You see if you can get one of them to confess. Meanwhile I'll see about getting a court order for those personnel records. I'll get it from a judge here and send it to the sheriff in Losgrove. He can serve it on Kathy Hull."

That sounded good to me, and I told Don I'd see what I could do about the confession, knowing that I'd handle things my own way in the long run.

"And by the way," Don said.

I hate it when people say that. Nothing good ever comes after it, so I didn't say anything. I just waited.

"I haven't had any reports from you," Don said.

I knew it wouldn't be anything good.

"This is a report," I said, but he didn't go for it.

"You'd better get everything down in writing. You can write it up and mail it to me this afternoon."

I needed a nap. "I don't think I could get it in the mail this afternoon. I'm pretty sure the last mail pickup's already happened."

"You'd better find out. I want a complete report on what's happened so far. Don't forget who's paying you."

"I'd never forget a thing like that," I said. "I'll send you the whole report as soon as I can get it ready."

"Good," Don said.

I hung up the phone thinking that I might as well do the report. I got my little portable typewriter out of its case. It took me quite a while to get everything written down, and, when it was done, I put all the pages in an envelope. I'd mail them as soon as I got a chance, but the first thing I was going to do was take a nap.

I put the typewriter back in its case and settled back on the bed, my head resting on a pillow about as thick as a Hershey bar. I was about to drift off to sleep when someone started pounding on the door.

At first I just lay there. I thought somebody had the wrong room. When the pounding continued, I shouted, "Who is it?"

"It's Joe Bronte. Open this door before I kick it in."

I sighed and got up, slipping my feet back into my shoes.

"Just a second," I said.

I walked over and clicked the deadbolt, then unlocked the door. Joe Bronte stood there red-faced and furious.

"What's up?" I said.

"You don't know?"

"I've had a long day, and I was trying to take a nap," I said, as if that would answer his question. "Why don't you tell me."

"A man's dead over at the tractor place."

"A man? Has he got a name?"

I figured it had to be one of two people, considering Bronte's attitude, and I was right.

"He has a name," Bronte said. "It's Wade Dickie."

"So why are you here?"

"Because you had a fight with him a couple of hours ago, and now he's dead. Let's go."

"Go where?"

"To the tractor place."

If he'd said we were going to the jail, I might have argued with him. But I was curious, and I might learn something, so while I'd rather have stayed there and taken my nap, I was willing to go to the tractor place with him.

"All right," I said, and I followed him outside.

CHAPTER 16

Bronte shoved the accelerator to the floor and peeled out of the motel parking lot with tires squealing. We blasted through the streets of Losgrove at high speed, not endangering anybody because hardly anyone was around. We hadn't gotten far before a state trooper showed up behind us. He would certainly have pulled us over if we hadn't been in a county car.

"You know him?" I said, pointing a thumb over my shoulder.

Bronte cut his eyes at the rearview mirror. "Yeah, that's Logan Farley. He's here to give us some backup."

"Us?" I said.

"You're the hotshot big-city investigator. I thought you might like to help us small-town boys out with this one."

"I must be missing something," I said. "I thought I was a suspect, and here I am, an honorary member of your department."

"You'd be a suspect if I didn't know where you'd been for most of the afternoon."

"You talked to Vivian?"

"She told me you had lunch and were at the café and stayed for quite a while. Then you went back to your room."

"Are you sure I didn't go by the tractor place and kill Dickie first?"

"I checked at the desk. You've been in your room the rest of the time, talking on the phone."

"They must be watching me closer than I thought," I said.

"You tell them to do that?"

Bronte didn't answer, but he didn't have to. I didn't resent his keeping an eye on me. He was just doing his job.

When we got to the tractor place, Bronte didn't stop in front. He pulled around to the side and drove around back. There was a big warehouse there that I hadn't seen before, and Bronte turned behind it.

There was a big crowd of people, fifteen or twenty of them, standing there. Bronte was going fast, and I was afraid for a second he might plow right through them, but he put a big foot on the brake, and the car slid to a stop.

Bronte was out of the car before I could even think. He started yelling immediately, shooing people away from the body that lay near the wall of the warehouse. By the time I got the door open and stepped out, there was nobody standing by the body except Kathy Hull.

She was distraught. Tears slid down her face as she turned to face Bronte. "It's Wade Dickie, Joe."

"I know who it is. You move away and get these people out of here. They're disturbing a crime scene, messing up footprints, leaving their own junk behind. Get 'em moved."

People were already getting well away, so Bronte was just giving Kathy something to occupy herself with, to take her mind off what had happened, and also to get her away from the body. She started talking to people, moving them farther away from the building. She didn't bother with me, and I stayed where I was.

Logan Farley came up beside me. He was a middle-aged guy with widely spaced brown eyes and a nose that had been broken sometime in the past. He was lean and almost as tall as I was. He looked good in his fitted uniform.

I introduced myself, and he shook hands with me. His grip was dry and firm.

"You working for the sheriff?" he said.

"I don't know," I told him. "I'm a private investigator from Houston, here on another case. But Dickie's involved in it."

"Dickie?"

"Wade Dickie. He's the one lying over there. You know him?"

"I don't think so."

"It was his house that a man named Percy Segal killed himself in a while back. Did you work that one?"

"Nope. The sheriff handled that one himself. Heard all about it, though."

That was all he had time to say because Bronte started to call out orders for him.

"Farley, you get some crime-scene tape up around here. Then get on your radio and call the county coroner. If there's anybody else you can think of that we need, call them, too."

"What about the state crime lab?"

"Me and the hotshot can work the scene, and Ellis is on the way. He can help out. We don't need the state lab for this one."

I wasn't so sure about that. I was pretty good, if not quite the hotshot Bronte kept calling me, but a state team would probably have been a big help.

"You sure?" Farley said.

"I'm sure," Bronte told him.

Farley shrugged and turned back to his car.

I could tell Bronte didn't like the shrug, but he ignored it.

"All right, Hotshot," he said, "let's me and you have a look at the body."

I could have done without the *Hotshot,* but I didn't say anything. Bronte probably hadn't meant anything by it, and, even if he had, there wasn't any profit in my mentioning it.

Dickie wore the same clothes he'd had on when I'd seen him earlier, blue work shirt, jeans, and some kind of off-brand tennis shoes that he'd probably bought at the local J. C. Penney store.

He lay on his stomach, his face turned away from us. I moved to where I could see it. His eyes were open, but he wasn't looking at anything. I saw where the gravel at the lumberyard had scratched the side of his face earlier, and I felt a little bad about that.

The scratches weren't bothering Dickie any, however. He was past being bothered by anything. There was blood all over the back of his blue shirt, where there were two big holes, and there would be more blood on the front, I was sure.

Bronte looked down at the body and made a clucking noise with his tongue. "Wade Dickie. Never thought I'd see him lying dead like this."

That was about as philosophical as Bronte was likely to get, and the mood didn't last long.

"What do you think?" he said. "Shot in the back?"

That one was too easy. Maybe he was testing me.

"I don't think so," I said. "Those holes are too big for that. They just about have to be exit wounds. I expect you'll find out he was shot in the chest. The bullets went right on through and blew out his back. He probably died immediately."

"All right. Anything else?"

"No shell casings," I said.

"Unless he's lying on them."

I didn't think so. I said, "How likely is that?"

"Not very," Bronte said. "I'd guess a thirty-two."

Again, maybe he was testing me. "I don't like to guess about things like that. Could be a thirty-two. Could be a thirty-eight. Or something bigger. Probably wasn't a twenty-two, though."

Bronte looked up from the body. "Another one of your jokes?"

"Just an observation. Are we going to wait for the coroner to get here before we move the body to have a better look?"

"Damn' right."

Kathy Hull had heard most of this conversation. She'd gotten everyone else to move well back, but then she'd drifted closer. She was standing almost where she'd been when we arrived. Her eyes were dry now, and she'd wiped the tears off her face. She was still plenty upset though.

She looked at me and Bronte, but it was the sheriff she spoke to. Her voice was rough with emotion.

"Do you think this has anything to do with what Ted is investigating?"

Farley came over then and asked us to move away so he could string the crime-scene tape. I thought it was too late, myself, considering that a dozen or so people had already trampled around all over the area, obliterating footprints, leaving their own trash behind when they moved away, and generally wreaking havoc with whatever evidence there might have been. I didn't mention any of that because it wouldn't have done any good and it might have made Bronte mad at me. I didn't need to get him any more stirred up than he was already. Besides, he might have thought of all that himself. It could have been why he didn't want the state's crime lab poking around. The scene was already too contaminated for them to be of any special help.

"What do you think, Stephens?" Bronte said. "You think this is related to what you're here for?"

Damned right, I did. Dickie was on my list. Segal, who'd started the whole "Houston Boys" deal, had killed himself in Dickie's house, and now Dickie was dead, almost certainly murdered unless there was a pistol lying under him. And I didn't think there was.

Again, I didn't say what I was thinking. Instead, I said, "I wouldn't know for sure. But let me ask you a question: How many murders do you have around here in, say, a year?"

Bronte came right out with the answer. He didn't even have to think about it. "Not many. We've only had three murders in the last five years."

"I didn't figure there'd be many in a town this size. Now let me ask you something else."

"Go ahead."

"How many of those were like this one?"

"What do you mean?"

"I mean how many of them were like on a TV show, with a dead body lying behind a warehouse and no shooter in sight."

Bronte waited a little while before he answered. He already knew what he was going to say, but he probably wondered why I'd asked that question.

I looked around while I waited. We were standing in a pathway or lane of hard-packed dirt behind the warehouse. Across the road was a vacant lot that hadn't been mowed in a while. The weeds had taken it over from whatever grass had been there. A couple of oak trees and a pecan tree towered over the weeds. The oaks had massive trunks and long limbs that stretched out over the weeds. They'd been there a long time, maybe since before there was a town.

On beyond the lot was a street, though there wasn't any traffic on it at the moment.

I looked back at Bronte, who still hadn't answered. We stood in the shade cast by the warehouse, but the shade didn't help much. The air was hot and muggy. There was no breeze to move it around, and it seemed to settle on us like a thick blanket.

"Well?" I said.

"I think I know what you're getting at," Bronte said. "Those three murders were all solved before anybody from my office even got to the scenes. All of them were honky-tonk killings, just a couple of drunks getting too feisty on too much beer, getting into arguments, and finishing things off with pistols. Well, pistols twice. Once it was a knife."

"So what would that lead you to think?"

"You don't have to get smart with me, Hotshot. I might be small-time, but I can figure things out if you give me long enough."

"Let me help you out a little more," I said, knowing I should have kept my mouth shut. I didn't want to stir Bronte up any more than I already had, but I was sure doing it. "What I'm investigating here is money obtained illegally, probably by insurance fraud. Bound to be some jail time involved with that for whoever did it. And then there's the possibility that somebody's been tampering with the mail. That's a federal crime. Maybe it's just a short step from those crimes to murder, and, if you're going to the old Graybar Hotel anyway, why not add murder to the list?"

"Be pretty stupid, for one thing," Bronte said.

"Yeah, but not everybody thinks it through like that. So maybe Dickie was killed because of what he knew about my case." I paused. "Or maybe some drunk came by and shot him for the hell of it. Take your pick."

Bronte snorted. "You know there's a lot of other possibilities."

"Sure there are. Like Percy Segal. He died in Dickie's house. I'm not supposed to talk about that, but it seems like a mighty big coincidence that Dickie's lying here now, don't you think?"

Bronte didn't answer, but Kathy Hull had something to say.

"Ted, do you still want my employee records?"

"Sure do," I said.

Kathy was tearing up again. "You can have them."

"Why the change of heart?"

"Because if what you're investigating is related to Wade's death, maybe they'll help you find out who killed him."

She started to cry, and Bronte surprised me. He pulled out a handkerchief from somewhere or other and handed it to her. If somebody had said he'd bet me a thousand bucks that Bronte had a handkerchief on him, I'd have taken the bet so fast it would've made his head swim. But there it was. Clean and white, too.

Kathy took it, thanked him, and wiped her eyes. He told her to go on to her office and said that we'd come by later and talk to her. She nodded and left, still sniffling.

"Farley," Bronte said.

The trooper came over. "Yeah?"

"You question all those fellas. See if they know anything useful. I doubt they do, but you never know. You mind doing that?"

"Not a bit," Farley said. He pulled a little notebook and pencil out of his pocket. "I'm ready to go."

"Get with it then," Bronte said.

Farley started toward the crowd of men.

"Time for us to look around here," Bronte told me. "Not that we're going to find much. Too damn' many people, and they've screwed things up."

We did look around, but we didn't find anything at all. No brass, no cigarette butts, nothing. Well, we found something that might have been footprints in the hard dirt, but they were indistinct and didn't mean anything. Any one of a dozen people could have made them.

The looking didn't take us long, and, by the time we'd finished, a car and a van pulled up behind Bronte's cruiser. Deputy Ellis was in the car. The county coroner and one other man were in the van. An ambulance stopped behind them. Now the crime-scene work was about to begin in earnest.

Chapter 17

The coroner was about as cheerful a man as I'd seen in a good while. I don't remember that he frowned even once the whole time I was around him. He was tall and skinny, with the kind of long fingers that concert pianists are supposed to have. His gray hair was thin and combed flat and close to his skull. He wore an open-necked white shirt, black pants, and black leather shoes.

He shook hands with Bronte and slapped him on the back. "What you got for me, Joe?"

"A dead man," Bronte said. "Wade Dickie."

"Wade Dickie? Isn't he the fella who owned the house where Perce Segal died?"

"One and the same," Bronte said, with a glance at me.

I didn't know how to interpret that glance, but it seemed to me that Bronte was maybe warning the coroner to be careful of what he said. I'm a suspicious sort, though, and maybe that wasn't it at all.

"This is Doctor Len Goldberg," Bronte told me. "County coroner. Len, this is Ted Stephens, a hotshot investigator from Houston, Texas. He's going to help me figure out who killed Wade."

I shook Goldberg's hand. His grip was cool and firm. Mine might have been firm, but I'd been outside too long for it to be cool.

"I'm no hotshot, Doctor," I said. "Just a guy who happened to be in town on a case."

"Call me Len. Have you worked homicides before?"

"A few."

"We don't have many in this county. Most of them are open-and-shut."

"I don't think this one is," I said.

"Maybe not. Let me have a look."

He slipped under the yellow crime-scene tape and took a long look at the body.

"What about me?" Ellis said. He was standing nearby, not having joined in the conversation with Goldberg. "Want me to help out Farley?"

"Good idea," Bronte said. "Stephens and I will work with Len."

Ellis nodded and went to join Farley. I had some ideas about what questions I'd like people to give the answers to, but nobody asked for my advice and I kept my mouth shut.

Goldberg was making a slow circle around Dickie, looking him over from all sides. Finally he stopped and called to the man who'd been in the van with him.

"Come on over, Willie."

Willie was the photographer. He wasn't much over thirty, and maybe younger. He had a mustache. I didn't like mustaches, but I figure the way a man grows his facial hair is up to him. Willie carried a couple of cameras, one Polaroid and one with regular film. He started taking shots of the body with the Polaroid. He knew his business, and Goldberg didn't have to instruct him in what to do.

When Willie was finished, he moved aside, and Goldberg called Bronte.

"Time to look in his pockets, Joe."

"Be right there," Bronte said.

He went to his cruiser and got a big plastic bag and a couple of pairs of surgical gloves. He stuck the bag under his arm while he snapped on a pair of the gloves, then walked over and handed the other pair to me.

"Put those on. You might have to touch something."

I took the gloves. They weren't easy to get onto my sweaty hands, but I managed it and went over to the body.

Bronte was already kneeling beside it. He pulled a wallet from Dickie's back pocket and handed it to me. I checked the money first. Twenty-nine dollars. A man couldn't get far on that. There was nothing else of interest, just a driver's license, a couple of credit cards, and a picture of two women, one of them about Dickie's age, the other much younger. His wife and daughter, I figured.

Bronte handed me the plastic bag. "Put the wallet in."

I did that, and Bronte gave me a handful of loose change.

"Here you go," he said.

I took the money and counted it.

"Ninety-six cents," I said and put it in the bag before Bronte could tell me to.

"Nothing in the shirt pocket," Bronte said.

"All right," Bronte said. "Turn him over."

I just stood there. I wasn't going to do his work for him, not after he'd called me *hotshot.*

"Little help," Bronte said, bending down.

Since he'd asked politely this time, and since he was going to do some of the work himself, I bent down and helped him turn Dickie's body over.

There was blood all over the front of Dickie's shirt, along with two small bullet holes. Bronte and I moved out of the way, and Willie started to take more photos.

Willie finished up his work, and Goldberg said, "Those holes in front are entrance wounds."

Bronte nodded without looking at me.

"Might be a good idea to look around for the slugs," Goldberg said.

Bronte looked over at the field. "Needle in a haystack."

Goldberg nodded and smiled.

"Might as well look, though," Bronte said. "Those bullets went right through him. Had to stop somewhere."

"That's right," Goldberg said. "Probably went through his heart, but I can't tell that without opening him up. Whatever they hit didn't stop them, though."

Bronte called Ellis over. "Farley doing all right questioning those fellas?"

Ellis nodded. "He should be. He knows his job."

"Yeah." Bronte sounded doubtful. "I want you to look in the field over there for the slugs that went through Dickie. Can you handle that?"

"Sure," Ellis said. "It's a good thing I brought the metal detector."

I thought he was joking, but he went to the back of his patrol car and opened the trunk. He took something out and closed the trunk lid. He looked back over at us and held up a metal detector.

"Your deputy's a smart man," I said.

"He is. Maybe smarter than me. He might even be sheriff someday." The sheriff was smarter than he let on, and he could have been right about Ellis. But I didn't think Ellis had a chance as long as Bronte was around.

"You got any questions?" Bronte said. Before I could answer he added, "About Wade Dickie, I mean. Not anything else."

"Now that you mention it," I said, "I do have a few questions."

"Let's hear 'em."

"Okay, here they are. Who was the last person to see Dickie? Was anybody with him within the last quarter of an hour before he was killed? Did he mention to anybody that somebody was after him? Had he argued with anybody lately?"

Bronte put up a hand to stop me. "Besides you, you mean?"

"I didn't argue with him. I helped him up after he fell, remember? I'm the good Samaritan here."

Bronte rolled his eyes behind his glasses. "Right. How could I have forgotten that? You got any more questions?"

"Hell, yes, I have some more. Did anybody hear the shots? Did Dickie say anything to anybody about any problems that he was having? Did he give any hint that something was wrong? Who found the body? Who called it in?"

I had some more, too, but Ellis yelled something from the field. I couldn't quite make it out, but then he yelled, "Both of 'em. I found both slugs."

He left the field and came over to me and Bronte. When he reached us he stuck out his closed hand.

"Show us," Bronte said, and Ellis opened his hand.

He was holding two mangled slugs. They looked like they might have come from a thirty-eight to me, but it was hard to tell because of their condition.

"I had to dig 'em out of a tree trunk with my knife," Ellis said.

Ellis hadn't had to use the metal detector to find them. Some bark was missing on the oak tree, and that had tipped him off. One of them was in bad shape, too mangled to do much good. After all, they'd gone through Dickie and hit a tree. One of them was in pretty good shape, however, and if we ever found the gun, a ballistics test could prove a match.

"Tag 'em and bag 'em," Bronte said, and Ellis went off to do it.

"Now about those questions of yours," Bronte said.

"I have one for Doctor Goldberg," I told him, and he called the doctor over.

"Ask him," Bronte said when Goldberg got to us.

"Doctor," I said, "how far away from Wade Dickie do you think his killer was standing?"

Goldberg shook his head. "No way to tell for sure right now. Probably no way to tell even later. We don't have a forensics lab here, but I don't think we'll need one in this case. What I can tell you is that there weren't any powder burns on Wade's shirt, which means whoever shot him was some distance away. I'd say fifteen feet or more. But that's just a guess."

It was an educated guess, though, and it was what I'd guessed, too. "How long's he been dead?"

"Not long. Postmortem lividity hasn't set in yet. After the heart stops beating, the blood settles in the—"

"The Hotshot knows what postmortem lividity is," Bronte said. "Right, Hotshot?"

"I sure wish you wouldn't call me that anymore, Sheriff."

There must have been something in the way I said it because Bronte looked at me a little funny. He said, "Sorry, Stephens. I didn't mean to piss you off."

"That's all right. But I'd like to drop it now. How old a man was Dickie?"

"In his forties," Goldberg said. "Why?"

"Just wondering," I said, thinking it was too bad that a man in the prime of his life could be cut down like that and left to lie in the dirt.

He didn't have to lie there much longer, however. Ellis directed the ambulance attendants while they loaded Dickie into their vehicle.

"We'll do an autopsy on him," Goldberg said, "but you already know the cause of death. We're not going to find anything different."

Bronte nodded, and Goldberg called Willie. They got into their van and left.

Farley had finished questioning everybody, which had been easy because nobody knew anything. Or if anybody did, nobody was saying. It had almost always been like that when I was a cop, and it wasn't any different now. Even when people could help you find out who'd killed someone or who'd driven away from an accident without stopping or who'd run out of a bank with a gun in his hand, they kept quiet. I don't know why. In their place, I'd have had plenty to say. I don't like it when people get away with committing crimes. But maybe that's why I was a cop.

Farley gave Bronte his skimpy notes, and Ellis went back on patrol. Everyone else had cleared out after Farley had talked to them, so that left me and Bronte. I started to ask him a few more questions, but he wanted to go inside.

"Too damn' hot out here," he said, and we headed for the main building.

We didn't get far before I saw Gail Cole and a short, stocky woman coming in our direction. Both women were crying.

"You wait here," Bronte said, and he walked ahead of me toward the women.

When he got to them, he said something that was too low for me to hear. Gail looked at me and then away before she and the other woman went back into the building.

Bronte turned around and waved for me to come along. I did, but I didn't like what I was thinking.

"Who was that with Gail?" I said when I reached Bronte, though I thought I knew the answer.

"Just some woman who heard about the shooting and came by to see if she could help out," Bronte said.

"So it wasn't Mrs. Dickie?"

Bronte didn't even blink. "What makes you think that?"

"They way they were carrying on. She didn't seem like just

some casual acquaintance, and Gail told me they were best friends."

"People around here don't have to be best friends to grieve together. People in Losgrove take care of each other. That's the way it is in a small town, but then you city boys might not know about things like that."

"We know about a lot of things," I said. "You might be surprised. I thought we were going inside where it's cool."

"Yeah," Bronte said. "Let's do that."

Chapter 18

When we got inside the tractor place, Gail and the other woman were already gone. It was then that I decided for sure: Bronte had lied to me, and the woman with Gail was Mrs. Dickie. I wasn't sure why he'd lied, but I was beginning to think there were a lot of things in Losgrove he didn't want me to know about. Maybe he didn't want anybody to know about them.

It was too bad, because I'd thought I could get along with Bronte, and I didn't like being wrong about somebody. I decided then and there that I was going to find out what happened to Percy Segal and Wade Dickie, even if their deaths didn't have anything to do with my case, though I believed they did. I think Bronte knew it, too, but he was trying to keep me from investigating. He hadn't had much luck at that, and he was going to have even less from now on.

Not that I was going to tell him so.

I looked around the room. A couple of men were behind the counter, but they didn't have any customers. Kathy Hull sat at her desk. A man sat in a chair beside the desk, talking to her.

"Who's that?" I said.

"Ed Holt," Bronte said. "He's the one who called in about Dickie."

He hadn't mentioned that earlier. Holt was one of the Houston Boys.

"I want to talk to him," I said.

"Be my guest. I'll be giving him a ride to the jail, and you can sit in on our interrogation if you want to."

I didn't want to. "I'll just ask him a couple of things while I'm here, if that's okay."

Bronte nodded, and went over to the counter to talk to the men there. I walked over to the desk.

Kathy Hull, who was dry-eyed now, didn't waste any time. She handed me a manila envelope and said, "The names you wanted are in there."

I took the envelope and thanked her. Then I introduced myself to Holt. Like a lot of people in Losgrove, he didn't look happy to see me.

When I told him I had a couple of questions, Kathy said, "I'll just leave you two here to talk," and she joined Bronte at the counter. I sat down in her chair.

"I hear you called in the murder," I said.

Holt stood about five-ten and seemed to be in pretty good shape. If he'd injured himself while he was working in Houston, you couldn't tell it by looking. His face was round and jowly, and he was sweating, even though it was cool enough where we were. He nodded in answer to my question but didn't say anything.

"I was wondering how you knew Wade was back there behind the warehouse," I said.

Holt mopped at his face with his hand and said, "I was in the can."

I must have given him an odd look. He said, "It's in the warehouse. Kind of out of the way, but that's where it is. Well, there's a restroom in here, too, but they don't like us to use it. We're usually pretty dirty."

I didn't see any point in pursuing that line of thought. I said, "What did you do when you heard the shots?"

"I finished my business, and then I went out back to see what was going on. I thought maybe it was just some old tractor backfiring, but there was Wade. So I came back here and called Joe."

"You stayed here until now?"

"That's right. I didn't see any need in bothering with a dead man."

"Did you see anybody out back when you went to look?"

"Just Wade."

"You look around any?"

"Nope. Soon as I saw Wade with that blood on him, I knew something was bad wrong. I didn't even get close to him. I ran in here and called Joe."

He didn't look much like a runner. I had a feeling he hadn't run very fast if he'd run at all.

"You didn't try to help out old Wade?" I said.

"He looked like he was beyond help to me. Too much blood."

I didn't see how he could have told Wade was dead, but maybe he was just squeamish. Or maybe he didn't care for Wade and didn't want to help him.

"You're one of the Houston Boys," I said.

"The what?"

"The Houston Boys. You went to Houston for a while and worked on the Ship Channel. Got hurt and came back home."

"I hurt my back," he said. He put a hand behind him as if to show me where his back was. "Slipped when I was trying to pull over a bale of cotton on a dolly. Man, that hurt. I was in bed for a week, couldn't move an inch."

"You're all right now, though. Working here at the tractor place, able to run in here to report a murder."

"I know what you're thinking, but you're wrong. I'm in pain all the time. I have to take pills four times a day just to keep moving. I don't do any heavy work."

"You're not disabled, though."

Holt stood up, pushing back his chair. "I'm going with the

sheriff now. I don't have anything else to say to you."

I stayed right where I was. "I'll see you later."

"Not if I see you first," he said.

He was almost as funny as I was. I watched him waddle over to the counter and say something to Bronte. Bronte nodded and came over to me.

"I'll handle the investigation from now on," he said.

At least he didn't call me *Hotshot.* "Probably for the best. Holt's on my list, though. I'll need to find out some more from him about that."

"Not while I have him."

"No, you have county business with him. Mine's different. I can wait."

I wasn't so sure my business was any different from the sheriff's, but I figured that's what Bronte wanted to hear. He nodded again and left. Holt went out with him. I stopped at the counter and thanked Kathy again for the list of names. I was outside before I realized that Bronte hadn't offered me a ride back to the motel. That was all right. I could walk, and I wouldn't have wanted to be in the car with him and Holt. I didn't trust either one of them.

I was hot and tired when I got back to the motel. It had been a long afternoon, and I wasn't any too happy about what was going on.

Don Cogsdill wasn't happy either, not after I called and told him what had happened and what I intended to do about it.

"Dammit, Ted," he said, "have you forgotten who's paying your salary?"

"I know very well who's paying it," I said. "You won't let me forget it."

"I'm glad to hear it. That means I'm doing my job. You should think about doing yours. If you get in trouble with that sheriff and get thrown in jail, the company's not going to bail you out."

"I thought maybe my friends would do that if the company wouldn't."

"If you're talking about me, forget it. As your friend, I'll give you a little advice. Do what you were sent to Losgrove to do and get out of Dodge."

It was good advice, and I wished I could follow it. I really did. But Bronte had pissed me off. Just about everybody I'd met in Losgrove had pissed me off except Mississippi Vivian, and she'd tried hard enough. I wasn't going to let them off the hook.

"What if I can prove that both Segal's and Dickie's deaths had something do to with our case?" I said. "What if they're an important part of it?"

Don didn't answer for a while. Then he said, "That would be different."

Damned right it would be different. I started to tell him so, but he said, "Can you prove they're part of our case?"

Wouldn't you know he'd ask an inconvenient question like that?

"Not yet," I said.

Don sighed. I waited. He sighed again. I kept waiting.

After a while he said, "You're a real pain in the ass, Stephens, you know that?"

"One of my character flaws," I admitted.

"One of many. This is against my better judgment, but I'm going to let you have your way on this. Not that it would do me any good if I said you couldn't."

Truer words were never spoken.

"You go ahead and do whatever you want to," Don said. "Solve the murders, help out the local law, whatever you think is called for. You've always done good work for us in the past, and you haven't always been exactly conventional in your methods. I guess I shouldn't expect you to start now."

What could I say? Those words were as true as his previous ones.

"You'd better produce some results, though," Don said. "And fast."

"I will," I said.

"You're just saying that because you know it's what I want to hear."

True again. He was on a roll. Even at that, though, I meant what I said. I intended to produce results, and I didn't plan to waste any time doing it.

"Do you have anything at all to go on?" he said. "Or are you just pulling my leg?"

"Would I do that? That's a rhetorical question, by the way. I do have something to go on. Several things, in fact."

"You mean it?"

"I mean it," I said.

"All right, then. Get to work."

And that's exactly what I did.

The first thing I did was look over the lists Kathy Hull and Gail Cole had given me. Sure enough, all the names I'd expected to find were on one or the other of them. I could have called Don and told him. Maybe it would have cheered him up to know all the Houston Boys were working like able-bodied men, but I wasn't in the mood to cheer him up or even talk to him again for a while. Besides, it was time for me to have some dinner.

I hoped that Mississippi Vivian would be waiting tables at the Magnolia Café, and, sure enough, she was. After we went through the preliminaries, which took some persistence on my part, I ordered some fried catfish and hush puppies. Before she could leave the table, I said, "I need to talk to my confidential informant again."

She looked around. There were eight or ten other people, but I was in the most secluded booth.

"I'll talk to you," she said, "but first I want to hear about Wade Dickie."

If she thought I'd give her a direct answer, she was wrong. "You mean we can trade information?"

Her eyes narrowed behind her glasses. "I didn't say that."

"We can discuss it when you have a free minute."

"You'll tell me about Wade?"

"We'll see."

She stood there for a few seconds, but when she saw that was all she could get from me, she left. She didn't say anything at all when she brought the breaded catfish and hush puppies, along with a tall glass of iced tea, and neither did I. She rattled the dishes a little when she set them on the table, but that was all.

The catfish was as delicious as I thought it would be. I didn't even need any ketchup on it. Mississippi Vivian's voice had reminded me of this kind of meal the first time I'd heard her say a word. All that was missing was the fried okra on the side.

I'd about finished eating when Mississippi Vivian showed up again, and not just to give me the check, though she laid that on the table, too, just as she sat down.

"I have a few minutes," she said. "Tell me about Wade."

"He's dead."

"I know that. I want to know what happened."

"I'm surprised you haven't already heard all about it."

I think it dawned on her about then that I was giving her a little of her own medicine. Her mouth set in a hard line, and she leaned back in the booth, glaring at me over the tops of her glasses.

I grinned and took a drink of tea. When I set the glass down, I said, "I need some information, and I need straight answers.

I'll trade you the Wade Dickie story, plus you'll get another payment. How's that?"

I could tell that the idea of another payment appealed to her. She'd been angling for that all along. She said, "I've heard some things about Wade, but I don't know what's true and what's not. You know how it is. People tell all kinds of stories, and it's hard to know which one's true. I want to know the straight of it."

"I can give you that. Do we have a deal?"

She nodded, and I told her most of the story, without any of my questions and without any speculation.

"I just can't believe it," she said, shaking her head. "First Perce and now Wade. It doesn't seem possible."

"Wade didn't kill himself," I pointed out. "Now I wonder if Perce did."

I'd been wondering that for a good while, but Mississippi Vivian stuck to her story.

"That's what Joe Bronte said happened."

I didn't tell her what I thought about Joe Bronte. I said, "Tell me about Johnny Turner."

She opened her mouth, and I thought she might be about to tell me something, but she didn't. She closed her mouth and smiled.

"That wasn't the deal," she said. "You mentioned a payment."

"You're going to get rich off me," I told her. "And my boss is going to complain about all the money I'm spending on informants."

"He thinks there's more than one?"

"He hasn't asked, but then I haven't turned in an expense account. Are you sure you can't give me this one for free?"

"Can't do it."

I hadn't expected anything different. I got a bill from my wallet as surreptitiously as possible and slid it across the table to her. She made it disappear into the big pocket on the front of her apron and patted the pocket in satisfaction.

"What do you want to know about Johnny?" she asked.

There were a lot of things I wanted to know. I hadn't asked Bronte about him, and I didn't intend to. Let Bronte figure it out on his own, if he could. He had the same information I did.

"As far as I know," I said, "Johnny Turner was the last person to see Wade Dickie alive. I'd appreciate it if you kept that to yourself, though. I don't want everyone in town knowing it."

"They'll find out," she said, "but if they do, it won't be because I told 'em."

I believed her. "That's good enough for me. Maybe Turner even knows what Wade was doing at the tractor place. I'd like to talk to him about that, but first I want to know something about him."

Sure enough, Vivian couldn't tell me without taking a sidetrack. "I heard you had a little tussle with him and Wade this afternoon. Seems like you whipped up on both of 'em."

News got around fast, all right, and this time it was accurate, not that I was going to admit it."

"Wade fell while he was loading a truck," I said. "All I did was help him get up."

Mississippi Vivian grinned. "Right."

"And even if it didn't happen exactly like that, I didn't kill Wade. The sheriff's sure of that, so you can rest easy."

"I never thought you killed him. I think I know you better than that. I don't think you'd ever kill anybody."

She didn't know me very well at all. I'd killed more people than I like to think about, and, even though that was in a war, it still bothered me at times. I even dreamed about it when I was having a bad night. But if Mississippi Vivian wanted to think I was a harmless old coot, that was just fine with me. I asked her again about Turner.

"He's a good kid, as far as I know. Played football on the Bobcats a few years ago. Bobcats, that's the Losgrove High team. Did well enough, scored a few touchdowns, but he wasn't a star. Didn't go to college because he wasn't that good, and his grades weren't that good, either. So he stayed right here in town and got a job at the lumberyard. Goes to church most Sundays."

"Is he sweet on Kathy Hull?"

"He might be. She's a nice young woman, even if she is too old for him. He hangs around the tractor place when he's not working. He used to go out with Barbara Dickie, though. She's the one he was sweet on."

Well, now. The elusive Barbara Dickie. I wondered where she was, why she'd left town, and what it might have to do with Johnny Turner. Among other things.

"Did he and Wade get along?" I said.

"Were they getting along when you saw them today?"

We were back to the kind of conversation I was accustomed to having with Mississippi Vivian, but she had a point even if she hadn't expressed it. The two men had seemed like pals to me, and Johnny had been plenty willing to help out Wade in the little scuffle we'd had earlier. Of course that might have been because Johnny didn't like me, but it seemed more like he was helping out a friend. Or trying to. He hadn't done too well at it.

"So you don't think Johnny's the reason Wade's daughter left town?"

She thought about it for a while, then shook her head. "I don't *think* so, but it seemed to me Johnny was the best thing ever happened to her. I might've mentioned that she was a little wild."

I nodded.

"Well, she calmed down a lot when she and Johnny started going out. He steadied her, and a lot of folks thought they'd get married. Then she left."

I recalled our earlier conversation. "Right after Percy Segal died."

"That's right. Couldn't live in the house where it happened, I guess."

I decided right then that I needed to have a long talk with Johnny Turner, but I had a few more questions for Mississippi Vivian first.

"Let's talk about Ed Holt a little bit," I said.

"The one who found Wade's body."

"Yes. What do you know about him?"

"Plenty. He grew up here in Losgrove, and we're about the same age. He was a year behind me in school. Didn't play football. Doesn't go to church."

"How did he and Wade get along?"

"Just fine, far as I know. They didn't exactly hang out together, but they were friendly enough the times they were here in the café."

I wondered if Joe Bronte was through questioning Holt. From the way Holt had talked to me, he wouldn't have had much to say.

"He worked in Houston for a while," I said. "You know anything about that?"

"Lots of people from here worked there for a while. They didn't like it there and didn't stay long."

"They all got hurt on the job."

"So you tell me. As far as I know, they didn't. They all seem to be just fine to me."

To me, too, and that was the problem, at least as far as Don Cogsdill was concerned.

"I think I'll drop by Johnny Turner's house and talk to him," I said. "Can you tell me where he lives?"

"Still lives with his mama and daddy. Little white house way out on Fifth Street. It's not even in the city limits, so it's not really on Fifth, but they call it that, anyway."

I didn't have a map of the town, but I thought I could find Fifth Street. The café was on Eleventh. I couldn't get lost in six blocks.

Mississippi Vivian agreed. "You'll need to go west when you get to Fifth. Turn left. Be sure you don't go the wrong way."

"Why's that?"

"Wrong side of town for a man your color."

"Mississippi," I said, and I wasn't using her name.

"You could say that. Things are different from the way they used to be. We even have a black man as a sheriff's deputy now."

I nodded. "I've met him."

"Not everybody was happy when Joe hired him."

She looked around the café, and I got the message. There wasn't a black face in sight.

"It's going to take a while," I said.

"Too long for some, not long enough for others. It's a hard thing." She paused. "Be that as it may, you don't need to be going to the East Side. People there wouldn't take kindly to seeing you. And just keep going along Fifth. You'll come to Johnny's house about a mile after you pass the city-limits sign. You be careful."

"I'm always careful," I said.

I figured I had plenty to worry about without stirring up any trouble on the east side of town. As it turned out, I had even more to worry about than I realized.

Chapter 19

The summer days are long in Mississippi, but it was just about dark when I left the café. I didn't mind. I thought I could find Johnny Turner's house without any trouble even after dark, and the heat let up a little when the sun went down.

I drove the rental car, a black Ford Falcon, through the quiet little town. A drugstore was still open, and all its lights were on, but as far as I could tell there were no customers inside. Everything else was already closed for the night. I figured the drugstore wouldn't be open much longer, either. There were only a few other vehicles on the street, a couple of cars and some old pickups that weren't far from antiques.

Following Mississippi Vivian's directions, I turned left on Fifth Street and found myself passing a car dealership and a hardware store. I crossed over some railroad tracks and drove past a feed store with a big red-and-white checkerboard Purina sign painted over the double doors. I passed a couple of ramshackle houses with yards that had more weeds than grass. On the front porch of one of them was an old car seat. Then I was out of town, though not officially. I still hadn't seen the city-limits sign. Like most places, Losgrove put those as far out as possible so as to collect city taxes from all the people they could provide with city services.

The pavement was cracked and crumbly along the edges, and occasionally a pothole showed up in the headlight beams. I drove slowly, just taking my time. I wanted to see the sights, such as they were, and I wasn't in any hurry to get to the Turner place. Even if Johnny and his folks went to bed early, they were likely to be up for a while longer.

The moon was coming up over the tops of the big oaks hung with Spanish moss in the wooded areas beside the road. If I'd seen a big plantation house like something from *Gone with the Wind,* I wouldn't have been surprised, but there was nothing like that around Losgrove. I suspected there were some cotton fields, however. Maybe I'd see a few of them.

I must have been dawdling along too slowly for the guy behind me in a rickety old pickup that needed a new muffler. It rumbled past me and on down the road before disappearing around a long curve.

When I rounded the curve myself, I saw a cotton field off to my right. A dirt road angled off to the left among some oaks and pecan trees, and ahead of me past the cotton field was a house that I assumed must belong to the Turners even though I still hadn't seen a city-limits sign. I saw lights on in the house and knew I'd get there in plenty of time to have my talk with Johnny.

Or I would have gotten there except for one little thing. The rumble of the muffler gave me all the warning I had, and then the old pickup that had just passed me came flying down the dirt road and out of the trees. Its lights were off, and it was headed right for me.

The driver had timed things just right. Because he'd been off the road, back in the trees, and because I hadn't been watching for him, there wasn't much I could do.

I floored the accelerator, and the Falcon didn't jump forward so much as shudder and lurch ahead a couple of feet. Next time I worked for Don Cogsdill and had to rent a car, I was going to demand that he pay for a Cadillac.

The pickup smashed into me. I don't know exactly what happened after that or the order things happened in. The noise of the crash was terrible: screaming metal, squealing tires, breaking glass. Maybe I was squealing, too, or screaming. I hoped I wasn't breaking.

Luckily, the Falcon had jolted just far enough forward so that the pickup didn't quite T-bone it. If that had happened, I'd have been mashed like a bug. As it was, I was still intact when the car spun around a couple of times and then flipped over.

And over. I don't know how many times it rolled because I was in no condition to count. I was bouncing around the passenger compartment like a BB in a bean can. I hit my head on the roof, the door, and maybe the floor, but never hard enough to knock myself out.

The Falcon, what was left of it, came to a stop, right side up, in the cotton field after plowing up a good bit of the cotton, which would have been ready for picking in a few more weeks if it had been left alone.

Both doors hung open, and the hood stood straight up in front of me. My head spun. The spinning was accompanied by a high humming noise, but I wasn't in any pain. That, I knew, would come later.

I looked to my left. The pickup was headed across the cotton field for the car. I couldn't hear it above the humming in my head, but I knew I'd better move fast. I flopped across the seat, rolled out the passenger door, and landed on my face. I got a snootful of dirt, and then I was up and running.

I got about twenty yards before my bum leg collapsed and sent me sprawling.

Behind me, the pickup crashed into the car and kept right on going, throwing dirt up from its back tires and plowing the cotton field with the Falcon, pushing it right at me.

I rolled to my left a few times, crushing cotton stalks as I tried to get out of the path of the Falcon.

I needn't have bothered. The pickup stalled and died before it had pushed the Falcon half the distance to where I was.

I lay there and tried to catch my breath. I hadn't carried a gun since I'd gone into the private-eye game. I'd never needed one. But I wished I had one now, not that it would have done me much good. My hands weren't steady enough to hold one, much less fire it accurately. I hoped whoever was in the pickup would give up and go away. Maybe he'd think he'd killed me.

It's never that easy, though. The humming in my head had diminished enough for me to hear a pickup door slam shut. Somebody was coming to check on me.

Or to finish me off. I didn't like that idea. I wasn't ready to be finished off.

I looked beyond the cotton field. There was a big stand of trees there, maybe a woods, deep and dark. If I could get there alive, I might be able to find a place to hide. I wondered if my leg would hold me up. I wondered if I could run even if it did. Only one way to find out.

I got up as quickly as I could under the circumstances and started to run, if you could call it a run. It was more like a controlled stumble. Running in a cotton field is a chancy business even on two good legs, and I thought I'd pitch forward on my face again any second, but I was going to get as close to the trees as I could before it happened.

The guy behind me wasn't as dumb as I was. He'd brought a gun to the party. I knew he had because he started to shoot at me. I heard the shots but not the bullets. I took that as a sign he wasn't a very good shot, but there was always a chance he'd get lucky.

Or maybe he didn't want to kill me with the gun. If I'd died in the car, it might have been written off as just another hit-and-run accident, but a dead body with a bullet in it was bound to be tied to the murder of Wade Dickie, especially if the bullet was from a thirty-eight.

I heard another shot, and this time the bullet buzzed by me like a bee. It occurred to me then that nobody ever had to find the body, not if it was buried somewhere. Deep within a dark woods, for instance. The thought almost brought me to a stop, but not quite. I might have a chance if I could get into the trees.

The next thing I heard wasn't a shot. It was the grinding of the pickup's starter. That meant there were two of them, one chasing me with the gun and one in the truck. All I needed was to have both a gunman and a pickup chasing me.

I stutter-stepped into the trees, my leg threatening to crumple at every step. The gunman couldn't have been too far behind me, though I didn't bother to look. I knew he couldn't have been running. A man can't run and shoot at the same time. It's hard enough to shoot while walking and in the dark to boot, so he'd probably had to stop each time he'd pulled the trigger, which meant he was a little way behind me.

It would take him another minute or so to get where I was, then, but he'd get there. What I needed was a place to hide.

What little moonlight there was didn't penetrate far into the woods. I could hardly see, which made running impossible. I shuffled as fast as I could, keeping my hands in front of me as I tried to find my way. The farther I could get, the easier it would be to hide, or that's what I told myself.

And then there was light. The pickup had pulled to a stop at the edge of the woods, and its headlights shone through the trunks and limbs, throwing shadows everywhere and lighting up my back, I was sure, like a target. I slipped behind a tree just before I heard the next shot and plunged deeper into the trees.

My leg was weakening. I fell twice within the next ten yards. I hoped I wouldn't have to kick anybody for a day or two, though I'd have enjoyed kicking the man with the pistol a couple of times, given the chance and two good legs. At the moment, however, I didn't have either one. Nor did I have a place to hide, but at least I was getting farther into the trees. The pickup's headlights weren't doing anyone much good now.

Then I fell into the hole. It wasn't deep, and it wasn't long, just a place that something had dug out around the base of a big oak tree. Maybe a feral pig had been after some acorns. It was deep enough for me to lie in, though, and it would be long enough if I pulled my knees up and tucked my head.

A dead branch lying nearby would cover me in the darkness. It wouldn't make me invisible, but it would have to do. I reached out, took hold of the branch, and pulled it over me. I lay on my side trying not to breathe as I waited.

It wasn't a long wait. The man with the pistol came along in a minute or so. He was breathing hard, and I heard a muffled curse as a tree limb swiped him across the face. The darkness and the branch hid me, and he went right on by me without so much as a pause, probably thinking that I was deeper in the woods.

I waited, hardly breathing, for a few seconds, just in case his friend had left the truck to come after me in the trees. When I didn't hear anyone else, I moved the branch aside and stood up. I leaned against the trunk of the tree to be sure I had my balance. I seemed to be okay, and the leg didn't wilt when I put my weight on it.

I had at least three choices. I could go after the man with the pistol, try for the guy in the truck, or sneak quietly away.

The third choice was the least attractive because I wanted to have a talk with somebody about what had just happened. I thought I could solve either my case or the sheriff's, or maybe both. And while I might not be up to kicking anybody, I wouldn't pass up the chance to give an opinion about the ancestry and sex habits of either one of those two bozos who was after me.

I decided the one with the pistol would be the best choice. He didn't have a flashlight, as far as I knew, so he wouldn't have any advantage on me.

I went after him. He was easy to track since he was blundering along like a blind rhino and cussing every time he bumped into something. His voice was still muffled and strange, as if he had something in his mouth.

Because I didn't have a gun and he did, I picked up a stick. It was about as thick as my wrist and a couple of feet long. It was also rotten, or it wouldn't have been lying on the ground, so it wasn't much of a weapon. However, it was all I had.

I don't know what tipped the man off that I was behind him. Maybe I was making even more noise than he was, or maybe he just felt that something was behind him. Some people have an instinct for that. It doesn't matter. Something warned him, and he whirled around.

A sliver of moonlight coming through the trees shone on his face. He looked like some kind of monster, his features distorted and flattened, and for a second I didn't move.

He was as surprised as I was, and I guess that's the only reason he didn't kill me right there. Well, the light was bad. That might have helped me, too, because while I was frozen in place, he snapped off a shot.

The bullet ripped my shirt and grazed my side. It burned like fire and brought me out of my brain-lock. There was only one thing I could do, and I did it. I threw my stick at him. I was too far away to do anything else.

I'd never claim to be a major-league pitcher, but I made a good, hard throw. And a lucky one. The stick flew at him end over end and hit him right in the middle of his forehead with a solid wooden *thunk.* He staggered backward and dropped his pistol. I jumped for it, but my leg betrayed me and collapsed as I made my dive. I slid forward on my belly and wrapped my fingers around the pistol grip.

The man growled and tried to kick the gun out of my hand. He missed and hit me in the head. Or maybe that's what he'd intended from the first. I was stunned but not out, so I rolled over and pulled the trigger.

The shot went wild, the bullet zinging off into the trees, but that was good enough. The man didn't fool around. He took off running, dodging in and out among the trees. I hoped he'd run into one, but if he did, I didn't see it.

I sat up and rubbed my head with my left hand. Rubbing it didn't make it feel any better. I scrooched over to a tree and stood up by bracing on the trunk.

By the time I was standing, I heard the pickup start. It rumbled away across the cotton field. I put my hand to my side and felt a sticky wetness. I didn't seem to be bleeding badly, so I started walking back the way I'd come.

I wasn't in a hurry, which was just as well, since I'd started to feel the bangs and bruises from the original collision, as well as the others I'd collected along the way since, not to mention the graze along my side. I was going to feel like hell in the morning, assuming I survived the rest of the night.

When I came out of the trees, I saw the hulk of the Falcon. I walked through the cotton field and fell into the front seat. I don't know why I bothered trying to start the car, but I did. No luck. I got out again and started toward the house I thought was the one where Johnny Turner lived. Maybe his folks would let me use the telephone.

Chapter 20

I hobbled out to the road, which was a little smoother than the cotton field, though the cracked pavement wasn't exactly perfect for walking. As I made my way along, I thought about the man in the woods. He must have had a stocking pulled down over his face, mashing his features flat. As a disguise, it had worked just fine. I hadn't recognized him, and I wouldn't know him if I ever saw him again. I had no idea who it was. It might even have been Joe Bronte, for all I knew. He'd lied to me, and he'd done everything he could to keep me from asking people about Percy Segal's death. Maybe he'd decided that the easiest way to shut me up would be to kill me.

I must have looked like a fugitive from a chain gang by the time I reached the Turners' front door. I knocked and waited. I could hear a TV set inside. Flip Wilson was yelling that the devil made him do it, whatever it was.

The porch light came on. The woman who opened the door almost slammed it in my face when she got a look at me. I didn't blame her. People should be careful about opening their doors, but, out there in the country, the Turners must have thought they were safe from anything that looked like I did.

"Ross!" she said.

I knew she wasn't talking to me, and in just a second she moved away from the door and a man took her place.

"What do you want?" he said.

He was a big man, broad-shouldered and narrow-waisted.

Probably about my age, but in a lot better shape than I was at the moment.

"Mr. Turner?" I said.

"Ross Turner, that's me. Who're you?"

I told him my name and said I was there to talk to Johnny.

"Johnny's not here." He gave me the once-over. "You look like you've been put through the wringer."

"I was in a wreck down the road. If I could use your phone, I'd like to call a wrecker."

He didn't open the door any wider. "I'll call." He looked at me more closely. "You want me to call an ambulance while I'm at it?"

"I'll be okay," I said, though I wasn't sure about that.

"Fine," he said, and shut the door.

I looked around the porch. There were a couple of metal chairs at one end, so I went and sat in one of them. A moth fluttered around the porch light, so I watched him for a while. I couldn't think of anything else to do. After about five minutes, the door opened and Mr. Turner came outside.

"I called the wrecker," he said. "I called the sheriff, too. He'll want to look into the wreck. You want some iodine for that little scratch?"

He pronounced it "eye-deen."

The bullet hadn't done much more than break the skin, but there was always the chance of infection, so I said, "It probably wouldn't hurt."

"Oh, it'll hurt, all right." He grinned. "I'll be back in a minute."

He went back into the house. When he came back, he had a bottle of aspirin and a jelly glass with some water in it. The glass had a picture of Yogi Bear painted on it.

Ross handed me the glass and the aspirin bottle. "You might want to take a few of these before I put the iodine on you."

He was right. I did want to take a few. I figured two wouldn't help at all, so I shook four of them into my hand and tossed them in my mouth. I took a couple of swallows of water and washed the aspirin down. It was probably just my imagination that the water tasted faintly of grape jelly.

I handed Ross the glass and the aspirin, and he disappeared into the house. While he was gone, I thought about the sheriff coming to investigate the "accident." He wouldn't be happy with me, but I'd already cooked up a story for him. More moths fluttered around the porch light, throwing their jittery shadows around. The moist heat of the night settled over me like a warm fog.

When Ross came back again, he was holding an iodine bottle, scissors, gauze, and tape.

"We'll get you fixed right up," he said, and he did. He was handy with the tape and gauze, and he was right about the iodine, though it didn't hurt so much as sting like the dickens. Being the tough guy that I was, I didn't yell. I might have twitched a little, however.

"Funny looking scratch to've been caused by a car wreck," he said when he was finished.

"You didn't hear it, did you?" I said.

"Hear what?"

"The wreck."

"Heard something. Wasn't sure what. We had the TV on."

I could still hear the faint sounds of Flip Wilson from inside the house.

"Johnny's not here, you said."

"Nope. He's sitting up at the funeral home with Wade Dickie. Didn't say when he'd be back."

People in small towns in the South still sat up all night with the bodies of departed friends. It wasn't exactly a wake. It was something that people had started doing back in the days when bodies were still kept at home before burial and when a cat or dog might wander in and do some serious damage. That wasn't going to happen at a modern funeral home, so the custom had long ago outlived any usefulness it might have had at one time. It hadn't died out, however, at least not everywhere. I should have thought of that.

"What you want with Johnny, anyway?" Turner said.

I told him again who I was and went on to explain who I worked for and what I was doing in Losgrove.

"Johnny can't help you with anything like that," Turner said. "He wouldn't know a thing about it."

"He's a friend of Wade Dickie's," I said. "He knew Perce Segal, too, I'm told. Both of them were drawing checks from the company I work for, and both of them were working jobs that injured men couldn't do. Maybe Johnny heard them say something about it."

Ross shook his head but didn't say anything. He didn't have to. I knew the headshake meant that Johnny wasn't a snitch.

I saw headlights coming down the road, and before long a wrecker pulled into the front yard. A big man wearing overalls and a welder's cap got out. He didn't have on a shirt. He shifted a cud around in his jaw, either tobacco or bubble gum. I figured the odds were good it wasn't bubble gum.

"Hey, Ross," he said.

"Hey, Bo."

Bo spit a long stream on the ground. Tobacco. "You got a wreck for me to pick up?"

"Down the road in the cotton field," I said. "You passed by it."

"Wasn't looking. Who's gonna pay me?"

"It's a rental. You can call the company."

I had the papers in my wallet. I pulled them out and gave him the information.

"I'll give 'em a call. What if they say they won't pay me?"

"I'm good for it." I told him which motel I was in. "I'll be here for a while longer."

He shrugged. "Guess I'll trust you."

He got back in the wrecker, and almost as soon as he backed and filled and got back on the road, a county car pulled in. The driver got out, and I saw it was Deputy Ellis. I was glad to see him instead of Bronte.

"Well, well," he said when he saw me sitting on the porch. "It's the outside agitator."

I grinned. It made my face hurt. I hurt all over now. The aspirin wasn't doing anything for me yet. I stood up and moved around a little on the porch so I wouldn't stiffen up.

"I'm the one getting agitated," I said.

"Maybe so. How are you this evening, Mr. Turner?"

"Tolerable. Where's Joe?"

"He's taking a little time off, so he sent me."

"You two go ahead and do what you got to do, then. I'm going in and watch TV."

I thanked Turner for his help. He nodded and left me and Ellis alone. Ellis told me he'd give me a ride to town.

"You'll have to give me a statement about the wreck," he said as I got in the car. "I have to write up a report on it. Was it a one-car accident?"

"Not exactly," I said, and I told him what had happened.

"So it wasn't just a run-of-the mill car wreck," he said after I'd barely gotten started.

"Not unless the other driver was drunk and blind."

"That's not impossible around here." Ellis grinned. "It's not even unlikely."

He stopped at the scene of the accident, and we watched Bo haul away the Falcon while I finished my story. Ellis and I got out of the car and looked around, but there was nothing there to help us figure out who'd hit me.

"You didn't recognize the pickup?" Ellis said.

"Never saw it before that I know of."

"What about the people in it?"

"I only saw one of them, the one who shot me. I couldn't tell if I knew him or not." I explained about the stocking mask. "You should be able to identify the pickup if you see it. The front of it should be dented up."

"You have any idea how many dented-up pickups there are around here?"

"This one might have some of the Falcon's paint on it."

"It might. It might be parked in a barn somewhere, too, and it might sit there for a few months."

He wasn't being exactly helpful. We got back in the county car and went to the jail, where he wrote up his report. While he was working on it, he let me clean up in the restroom, as best I could.

I didn't improve my appearance much, but I got most of the dirt off and combed the sticks out of my hair. Ellis had finished the report by the time I was done. I read over it and agreed that he had the facts down correctly.

"How about a ride to the funeral home?" I said. "My car's in the shop."

Ellis didn't crack a smile. If I'd thought he'd be the one to appreciate my jokes, I was dead wrong. He did give me a ride to the funeral home, though.

Chapter 21

The lighted sign out front said "Wilbanks Brothers Funeral Home & Chapel." It was an impressive place, an antebellum mansion, or what looked like one, with a wide porch, tall columns, and a broad, green lawn that in daylight would be shaded by the canopy of the oak trees that stood around here and there.

"Not bad," I said when Ellis stopped the car at the curb.

"Wouldn't know," he said. "My kind don't get buried out of there."

Things had changed in Mississippi, but they hadn't changed enough. It hadn't been much more than fifteen years since Emmett Till had been beaten, shot, and dumped in the Tallahatchie River. The killers had tied a gin fan around his neck with barbed wire, but it didn't keep him under. Till's crime was speaking to a white woman. He was fourteen years old. It would take a long time for people to get past things like that.

"I don't mind," Ellis said. He was talking about the funeral home, not Emmett Till. "We got our own place, just as nice."

I didn't suppose it mattered much, anyway, what kind of place it was, whether you were Emmett Till or the head of the Klan. When you were dead, you weren't likely to notice.

I got out of the car and thanked Ellis for the ride. As he drove away, I started up the walk to the front door. I hurt in pretty much every muscle and joint in my body, so I didn't exactly sprint. I told myself that when the aspirin kicked in, I'd be fine, but, at the moment, I had a serious hitch in my get-along.

I hadn't seen any cars parked along the street in front when Ellis let me out, but there were lights on inside the building. I assumed everyone had parked in back.

The porch had only a couple of steps, which was a good thing. I wasn't sure I could have climbed any more than that. I opened the tall front door and went inside, where I found myself in a hallway leading back into the building. Half of the hallway on the right was taken up by a staircase that went up to the second floor. The door on my left was closed, but a discreet sign let me know that the room behind the door was the chapel. The door on my right was open, and I heard laughter and loud talk coming from inside. I figured I'd come to the right place.

I stuck my head through the door and took a look. A bronze-colored casket rested on a stand at the front of the room. The top half of it was open. A floral spray lay on the bottom half. It was almost midnight, and I figured the morticians had been able to get Dickie embalmed and laid out by now, though I couldn't tell from where I stood.

The rest of the room was filled with men, most of whom were dressed no more formally than Bo the Wrecker Driver had been. My clothes were ragged and torn, but my face was clean and my hair was combed. I thought I'd fit right in.

I looked around to see if one of the men looked as if he might have been hit in the middle of the forehead by a stick. From where I stood, I couldn't see any bruises or bumps.

One reason for the noise and general hilarity had to be the contents of a number of Mason jars that were scattered around the room. Some of them sat on empty wooden folding chairs, and men drank from the others. The liquid in the jars was clear, but it wasn't water. I inhaled the powerful alcohol odor of Mississippi moonshine. White lightning.

Johnny Turner stood near the casket. His face was red, and he was laughing at something someone had said. The someone might have been Ed Holt, who was standing near him, talking to another man I didn't recognize. The only two people I knew other than Turner and Holt were John B. Campbell and Trooper Logan Farley.

I thought it was interesting that Farley was there. He'd given no indication that afternoon that he and Dickie were friends, and I wondered if it was appropriate for a state trooper to be drinking moonshine, especially one who was in uniform and wearing his sidearm. For he was certainly drinking. He had a jar of the stuff in one hand, and I didn't think he was holding it for a friend. I remembered that Bronte had appeared a little skeptical about him. Now I wondered what that skepticism was based on.

Everyone in the room, including Farley, seemed to have quite a buzz on, and nobody noticed me standing in the door until John B. Campbell turned around and caught a glimpse of me. He didn't say anything to anyone, but he motioned for me to go back out in the hallway. I did, and he came out to join me.

John B. was one of the few men wearing a jacket and tie. He must have put the tie on after business hours were over, out of regard for the dead. The tie was a little askew now, and Campbell's forehead was beaded with sweat even though the room was cool.

"What the hell are you doing here, Steve?" he said.

Since he called me *Steve,* I assumed we were buddies.

"I came to pay my respects," I said.

Standing there, John B. was just a little taller than my belt buckle. He shook his head and gave me a look that plainly implied I was crazy.

"Well," he said, "you better get out now, before anybody else finds out you're here. Wade hasn't been laid out in there more than fifteen minutes. They just now got him ready. But the drinking's been going on for a while."

"I don't see what that has to do with anything."

"Are you crazy? Johnny Turner's told everybody in there how you got into a fight with him and Wade this afternoon and how they whipped your butt. He's got them all believing you killed Wade to get back at them and that maybe he'll be next on your list."

"He really told them that?"

"What?"

"That they whipped my butt?"

"He sure did, and, from the look of you, I'd say he got it right."

"We did have a little scuffle, but that's not why I look like this. I thought a different story was going around about our little set-to."

"Yeah," John B. said. "I heard it different at first, but Johnny says that was all wrong. Says they cleaned your clock." He looked me over again. "If they didn't whip you, what the hell happened?"

"Car wreck," I said, stepping around him and entering the room.

He pulled on the back of my shirt, but not hard enough to slow me down, much less stop me. I walked through the crowd of men, sidestepping the folding chairs, and took a look in the casket. The body inside belonged to Wade Dickie, all right. The makeup job was a pretty good one, and maybe people would have said he "looked natural," though he was a little too pink, I thought. The suit coat he had on covered the bullet holes. I caught the faint scent of moth balls, and I was pretty sure he hadn't worn the suit often when he was alive.

A heavy hand landed on my shoulder. I turned and saw Johnny Turner.

"What the hell are you doing here?" he said. His breath could have peeled paint.

"You're the second person who's asked me that," I said. That was the second time he'd put his hand on me. I was getting tired of it, but I didn't want to cause trouble. "I'm beginning to think I'm not welcome here."

"Damn' right, you're not. It's your fault Wade's lying there dead."

People stopped their own conversations to listen. A couple of them edged closer.

"My fault?" I said. "I didn't shoot him. If I'd shot him, I'd be in jail, not here."

"I didn't say you shot him." Johnny leaned closer. I tilted my head back as far as I could, but I couldn't escape his breath. "I said it was your fault, coming to town and asking all those questions, stirring things up. I ought to knock your block off."

Nobody had said that to me since I was a kid, and I didn't really think Johnny could do it since he'd tried twice without any success. It was just the liquor talking, however, and I was willing to let him off the hook.

"I apologize if I've caused you any trouble," I said.

He didn't want to hear my apology. He turned to Ed Holt and handed him the Mason jar.

"Hold this," he said.

Holt took the jar, which meant that he now had one in each hand. He was the kind of man who looked perfectly at home that way.

"I'm gonna whip your candy ass," Johnny told me.

That was a little better than knocking my block off, but not by much. I glanced over at Farley, thinking that maybe he'd put a stop to things before they got out of hand, what with him being a lawman and all, but he was looking into his own jar as if there might be a bug floating around in it. Considering where the whiskey must have come from, I wouldn't have been surprised if he'd found one.

I wondered briefly where the funeral director was. It seemed as if he'd want to be there in case of trouble, but maybe he knew there'd be trouble with all the drinking and had decided that he didn't want any part of it.

For whatever reasons, nobody in the room was going to help me out. I'd have to deal with Johnny myself. I thought it would be best if I gave him another chance to leave me alone and save face with his friends, all of whom were now watching us closely, with at least three quarters of them, I figured, hoping for a good fight. I didn't know if they believed Johnny's story about what had happened that afternoon and wanted to see him whip me again, or if they didn't believe it and wanted to see for themselves what would happen if the two of us tangled.

"Just help me out here." I backed away. I wasn't going to let anybody say I started a fight. Well, they could say it, but I didn't want it to be the truth. "Tell me who perpetrated the insurance scam on my company, and I'll go away and leave you alone."

"You don't give a damn who pup—parp—pear—did that insurance scam," Johnny said, and then he swung at me.

Just as he had in the lumberyard earlier that day, he telegraphed the punch. This time he was drunk, so it was even easier to move out of the path of his fist. As his arm flailed past my face, I took hold of it and spun him around a few times.

That was a mistake because of the people who stood around us. As I whirled Johnny, his other arm flew out, and he struck some of the others. Mason jars hit the floor, and white lightning splashed on the walls. Anguished shouts filled the room. It sounded as if they mourned the loss of the liquor more than the loss of Wade Dickie.

I let go of Johnny's arm. That was my second mistake. In his condition, he had no sense of balance at all, and the spinning hadn't helped him any. He flopped around, loosey-goosey as a rag doll, and blundered over to the casket stand and fell heavily against it.

It was a little like watching a slow-motion movie. The stand tilted and teetered. For a second I thought it might right itself.

It didn't. It fell over, with Johnny sprawled across it. The bottom half popped open, dumping Wade out on the floor. He wasn't wearing pants. I thought that was a bit undignified. I knew it couldn't be easy to put pants on a corpse, but still.

Nobody noticed at first. Several fights had broken out because of spilled liquor and stained clothes, with everyone blaming everyone else for what had happened. It didn't take long, however, for them to focus on the real culprit. Me.

Holt was the first to get to me. His face was contorted with anger, and a faint red line ran down the left side of his forehead and cheek. He still held one of his Mason jars. Instead of throwing it at me, he tossed it back over his shoulder with his right hand and swung at me with his left.

He was a little faster than Johnny, and his fist grazed my chin. Before he could take another swing, I stepped forward and hit him right in the middle of his chest with the heel of my hand. I put a lot into it. He sucked a deep breath, or tried to, and staggered backward, running into Trooper Farley, who was wet and angry, having been hit by Holt's jar of hooch.

I'm pretty sure that Farley wouldn't have pulled his gun for crowd control under normal circumstances, that is, when he was sober. But, like just about everybody in the room except me, he'd had a bit too much to drink. So he pulled the gun.

Holt stood between me and Farley, gagging. He got some air now and then, but he clearly didn't feel too well. I was afraid he was going to heave up some hooch, but so far he'd managed to hold it down.

Farley grabbed him by the collar with his free hand and jerked him back and to the side, moving him out of the way.

That did it. Holt spewed. Some of it—a good bit of it, to tell the truth—got on Farley, who surely considered shooting Holt, but didn't. He did pull the trigger of his pistol, but I think that was pure reflex. The first shot spanged into the casket. The second one hit Wade Dickie in the side of the head. It didn't do much damage, but it did make a neat hole.

That brought things to a quick stop.

"Goddamn," somebody said, his tone hushed, almost reverent, "he shot Wade again."

People gathered around the body and stared. They all looked a bit sheepish, except for Turner, who was still sprawled on the casket, and Holt, who was bent over at the waist, both hands on his knees. I wasn't sure that he was through heaving, but the only thing he was likely to mess up this time was his own shoes.

The most sheepish of them all was Farley, who holstered his pistol and tried to pretend that nothing had happened.

A man in a black suit came into the room. He was undoubtedly the funeral director, and he wasn't happy.

"What's going on here?" he said.

Then he looked around. He appeared to be so shocked that I thought for a second he might faint.

"Johnny Turner tried to hit me," I said, since nobody else seemed willing to explain things. "After that, things got a little out of hand."

"A little?" the funeral director said. His voice rose. "A little?"

I waited for someone else to speak up, but no one seemed to have anything to say. I didn't mind talking, however. I wasn't shy.

"I just got here, myself," I said, "so I can't say for sure. But I think some of these fellas might have been drinking. I'll bet there's some kind of law against that. You might want to call the sheriff."

If there was anything he didn't want to do, it was to call the sheriff, and I knew it. He drew himself up and said, "I believe we can take care of things without that."

"It won't be easy," I said. "Your client's got another bullet in him."

The director looked at Wade, sprawled out on the floor. "Jesus Christ."

"Nope, just Wade Dickie," I said. "A little the worse for wear, though." I moved toward the door. "I'd stick around and help you clean up the mess, but I've had a hard day. I'm going back to my room and see if I can get some sleep."

Nobody tried to stop me, so I left. I didn't know exactly where the motel was or how I was going to get there. I'd thought I might be able to get a ride with someone at the funeral home, but I now I didn't think asking for one would be a good idea. Anyway, it was a nice evening for a walk. It was warm, but the humidity wasn't too bad. There were only a few clouds, and I could see the stars. A few fireflies flickered across the lawn in front of the funeral home, reminding me of my childhood for some reason.

I started walking. I figured I could find my way easily enough, and I did. The business district was quiet, and I didn't see a single car on the streets all the way back to the motel. The walk even did me good. It worked out some of the soreness left over from the wreck and the fight in the woods, and it gave me some time to think over everything that had been going on. Some things had started to clear up for me, or I thought they had, but mostly they were still too murky for me to make sense of.

Nevertheless, it was a start.

Before I went to bed, I took four aspirins and phoned Sarah. She thought it was a little late for me to be calling.

"I've been busy," I told her. "Sometimes a case keeps me out later than I'd like."

"Are you all right? You sound a little funny."

"Just tired," I said. No use to worry her, and I was fine. Nothing wrong with me that a little aspirin couldn't take care of. "I'll be fine after a good night's sleep."

"Are you sure?"

"I'm sure," I said.

We talked a little longer, and, after I'd hung up, I lay down and went to sleep in seconds.

Chapter 22

The next morning I felt sore all over, so the walk hadn't helped as much as I'd thought. I took some aspirin and a long, hot shower, then went to the garage where the Falcon had been towed. The owner had notified the rental company, and he rented me another car, a Plymouth Fury, several years old and painted a sort of pea green.

"I hope you'll take better care of it than you did that Ford," he said. "Renting out a car's just a sideline for me. I don't do it as a general rule, so I don't have as much insurance as Avis and Hertz."

I told him I'd take care of his car and drove to the Magnolia Café for breakfast. If Mississippi Vivian was curious about my battered appearance, she didn't mention it. That was just as well. I figured she'd already heard a dozen or so different stories about my latest adventures in Losgrove, and I didn't feel like explaining things, not until I'd had something to eat.

When the breakfast rush was over, she came to my booth and said, "You really have stirred things up in our little town."

"I didn't intend to," I said. I felt better with some eggs and sausage inside me. "I just wanted to do my job and leave."

"Your job has gotten all mixed up with other things, from what I hear. You'd be a lot better off if you just stuck to the job and forgot the rest."

"Do you know something you need to tell me?"

"Why would you think that?"

"I don't know. Maybe because you implied it."

She looked at me over the tops of her glasses. "As much as I hate to say it, you've lost yourself an informant. I liked the money, but I have to live here after you're gone back to Houston. From now on, I'm keeping my mouth shut. I think you're okay, but I'm about the only one in town who does. You're on your own."

"What happened at the funeral home last night wasn't my fault."

Mississippi Vivian grinned. "I don't know if it was or not, but I wish I could've seen it."

"It probably wasn't nearly as interesting as the stories you've heard, whatever they are."

"I guess I'll never know."

"Believe me, you don't need to," I said.

"How about the car wreck?" she said. "Was that interesting?"

"Very. But, as you can see, I don't have a scratch on me."

"Sure enough. And you don't hurt a bit. That's why you eased down on that seat like you'd jump a foot if it touched you in the wrong place."

I'd thought I looked pretty nimble. I must have been mistaken.

"I'm fine," I said. "I just need to work a little of the soreness out. You sure you don't want to be my informant anymore?"

She nodded.

"Well, since you won't talk to me, I'd like to talk to Mrs. Dickie. Maybe she could help me out."

"With your job or with something else?"

I tried to look innocent. For me, that's not easy. "What else could there be?"

"You know what else. Anyway, she won't talk to you. Nobody in town will. You'll be lucky if Joe Bronte doesn't lock you in the hoosegow."

I'd thought about that last night, but when nobody showed up with cuffs this morning, I'd stopped worrying. After all, I hadn't done anything. Joe Bronte might not see it that way, but he knew he couldn't get away with locking me up.

"Anyway, Mrs. Dickie's grieving," Mississippi Vivian said. "Even if she'd talk to you, you shouldn't be bothering her. It's not right."

Lots of things weren't right, including a few in Losgrove. I couldn't let Mrs. Dickie's grief stand in the way of my finding out those things, some of which were related to my job. It wasn't pretty, but there it was.

I thanked Mississippi Vivian for the advice and drove back to the motel, where I looked up Wade Dickie's address in the phone book. I wrote down the address and spiffed up a little. I didn't have a suit with me, but I wanted to look as nice as I could when I made my condolence call.

The Dickies' wood-frame home sat on a sleepy street of houses that looked as if they'd all been built in the early part of the century. I had to park several houses away because cars lined the curb in front of the house. Tall pecan trees shaded the walk to a wide front porch made of concrete. The brown grass of the lawn could have used some water.

A couple of men stood on the porch, smoking cigarettes and talking in low voices. I didn't know either of them, and I didn't remember them from the funeral home. I kept my head down, anyway. They might not have let me pass if they'd known who I was. As it was, they gave me some odd looks, and I figured they'd eventually work out where they'd seen me. I wove my way through them, looking at my feet, nodding, and mumbling something that could pass for a greeting. They didn't try to stop me.

The front door opened right into the living room. On the left was a couch, where Mrs. Dickie sat. Next to her was a young woman who, though slender, looked very much like her. She had to be Barbara, the daughter. Both women were red-eyed and sad. Stout women sat beside them with their arms over their shoulders. Other women flocked around, all of them in their Sunday best, floral dresses and shoes with a little heel. No black dresses yet. Those would come out for the funeral.

Across from the couch, French doors opened into a small dining room. The table was covered with casserole dishes, salad bowls, pie plates, all filled with food that the women had brought to the house.

The hum of conversation dimmed and died when people saw me standing there.

"My name is Ted Stephens," I said. "I've come to pay my respects to Mrs. Dickie and her daughter."

"Humph." One of the women on the couch stood up and confronted me. "We've heard of you, Mr. Stephens, and you're not welcome here."

"Maybe not," I said, "but I think Mrs. Dickie should be the one to tell me that."

She looked up at me. "You're the one my husband beat up yesterday?"

Let her think what she wanted to. "Yes, ma'am, that's me. He had help, though."

She nodded. "Johnny Turner. He got into some trouble last night at the funeral home. That was you, too."

I looked at Barbara and said, "I hope he's not hurt."

Barbara's hands were in her lap. She looked at them and said nothing.

Her mother said, "Maybe you and I should have a talk, Mr. Stephens."

"Good idea. Can we go somewhere else to have it?"

She heaved herself up and off the couch. "The kitchen. You

come, too, Barbara."

Barbara looked up then. She shook her head to indicate that she wasn't moving. Mrs. Dickie didn't say a word. She reached down, took one of Barbara's hands, and pulled. Barbara stood up. She must have known better than to resist. Mrs. Dickie looked at me and started toward the dining room. Barbara followed, and I was right behind them. The women glared at me but didn't speak.

The food on the dining table smelled good, even so soon after breakfast, but we didn't linger there. The next room was the kitchen. It was small and crowded with a breakfast table and three chairs. One side of it was against the wall.

"You want some coffee?" Mrs. Dickie asked.

You could trust a Southern woman to be polite under any circumstances. I looked at the tall chrome percolator on the counter by the sink. The coffee smelled good, but I said, "No, thanks."

"We can sit down, then," Mrs. Dickie said, and I pulled out a chair for her.

I can be mannerly myself when the situation calls for it, and she gave me an appreciative look. Barbara seated herself and stared down at the table. I wondered if she knew that she was the one I'd most like to get some answers from.

I took a seat at the table, trying not to show that I was a little sore. I was sure I did better than I had at the café.

"You came to town about some insurance thing," Mrs. Dickie said. "You think Wade was involved."

I liked people who got right down to the topic at hand.

"Yes, I do, but that's because of his association with a man named Percy Segal."

"Perce," Mrs. Dickie said. It sounded like a curse word.

"That's the man. I take it you weren't fond of him."

Barbara squirmed in her chair.

"He killed himself in my house," Mrs. Dickie said. "What good can you say about a man like that?"

"Very little. He's the one my company believes started an insurance scam in Houston. He filed what we believe was a false claim. So did a lot of other men from Losgrove. One of them was your husband."

"Wade would never do anything crooked like that."

I hadn't brought my briefcase because I'd been afraid no one would let me in if I looked like some kind of salesman. So I couldn't offer her any proof. I assured her that I had it, however.

"I don't believe you. Perce Segal was a crook and a scoundrel, and I'm not sorry he's dead. He's the one to blame."

It's always easy to blame the dead for your troubles. There's not much they can do to refute you. Not that I didn't agree about Perce Segal. I suspected she was right about him, but I also thought Wade Dickie was in on the scam. I'd considered everything pretty carefully last night, and I believed that Wade and Perce might have been the instigators of the scheme and that they must've had a falling out. I wasn't sure what the falling out might have been about, but my conclusion was that Wade had killed Perce because of it.

Or maybe not. Another theory I came up with was that Johnny Turner had killed Perce because Perce had made a pass at Barbara. He had the reputation for that kind of thing, and Johnny had a bad temper and was quick to act on it. For that matter, Wade might have killed Perce for the same reason.

Somehow others had to be involved as well, including John B. Campbell or maybe his secretary, Carolyn Lacy. The mail came into that office, and they had to know about it. There was another possibility about the mail, however, one that I hadn't explored yet. I intended to get to that later in the day.

Wade Dickie's death figured into everything, but I still wasn't sure how. I didn't know who'd killed him, but I had what I thought was a pretty good idea. That was another thing I'd need to investigate, if the sheriff didn't beat me to it. It might lead me to the answer to my insurance scam, or it might not.

All those ideas were running around in my head, and I just needed to get them into some kind of order. I thought maybe Barbara or her mother could help me.

"Perce is the one I'd like to talk about," I said. "If it's not too painful for you. I'd like to know how he came to kill himself here in your house."

"It wasn't in the house, exactly," Mrs. Dickie said. "It was on the sleeping porch."

I hadn't really noticed before, but a door from the kitchen led to a screened-in porch. It could have been used for sleeping in warm weather, but I didn't see any beds. Not even a cot. Anyway, I didn't think it mattered where he was killed.

"You were working at the time it happened, I believe," I said.

"That's right. I was at the drugstore."

"What about you, Barbara?"

Her mother answered for her. "She wasn't here. She'd been staying with a friend for a while, and after it happened, she moved out of town." She patted Barbara's hand. "I'm glad she's back now, though. I need her."

Barbara didn't look happy to be back, but under the circumstances you couldn't blame her. She also didn't intend to talk to me, so I decided to push her a little.

"I hear you and Perce got along pretty well," I said. "He was a real ladies' man."

Barbara flinched. "He was a pig, a greasy, sweaty—"

She didn't get to finish the sentence because who should come banging in through the screen door on the sleeping porch but Mississippi Vivian. She carried a metal pan covered with foil in one hand. I smelled meatloaf.

"Brought this over from the café," she said, setting the pan on the counter by the percolator. "What are you doing here, Ted?"

She knew what I was doing there well enough, so I didn't say anything.

"I think it's time for Ann and Barbara to let their friends comfort them," she continued. "You might as well go on now, Ted."

She hustled Barbara and her mother out of their chairs and into the dining room before I could protest. As she passed through the doorway, she looked back at me and smiled as if to say she'd told me not to bother the Dickies but had known I would. Now she thought she'd thwarted me, but I'd picked up on a thing or two before she'd arrived.

I gave her a smile in return. I didn't say a word to the women in the living room or to the men on the porch, and nobody spoke to me, either.

Chapter 23

Like everything else in Losgrove, the post office wasn't hard to find. It was a square, red-brick building about a block down the street behind John B. Campbell's office. My next step was to find out something about the mail handlers in Losgrove.

If John B. and Carolyn Lacy had both told me the truth, they didn't know a thing about the letters containing the checks mailed out to the claimants by the National Insurance Company. If they were lying, well, I'd have to do something about it, and I figured one way to check up on them was to find out about the mail delivery. It was possible, after all, that the checks never arrived at John B.'s office.

There was another possibility, too. Since Carolyn wasn't always there, and since John B. was in his office where he couldn't see the secretary's desk, someone could have come in off the street and taken the letters. That didn't seem likely, but I couldn't rule it out, not yet.

I liked to think I knew a little bit about people, and, though I'd often been fooled, I was pretty sure that John B. and Carolyn had told me the truth. And I didn't really think anyone could time it so that every single month he could get into the lawyer's office and swipe the mail right off Carolyn's desk without anyone ever knowing.

That left the post office. The letter carrier would be the person with easiest access to the mail, so I thought I'd have a talk with the postmaster about my problem. Having the talk wasn't easy, though, because the postmaster didn't have anything to say to me, especially after I told him what the problem was.

"That's federal business," he said, and he folded his hands on his desk. "It doesn't have anything to do with you."

He was a trim little man with a brush cut hair shot with gray. He was the only man I'd seen in town who wore a sport coat and tie to work. His name was Aubrey Stokes, and his office was as neat as he was.

"It's the company's money," I said. "That makes it my business. If somebody here's taking the money, I need to know about it."

"Now that you've informed me about the problem, I'll look into it," he said. "I'm sure the Postal Inspection Office will send someone to investigate as soon as I notify them." He looked at the National Insurance business card I'd given him. "I promise you I'll let your company know what we find out."

I talked with him for a bit longer, but he didn't give me any information, and he didn't say anything remotely helpful. The letters were his job now, and, if something crooked was going on in his post office, he was going to take care of it. As far as he was concerned, I was out of the picture.

I thanked him for his help as if he'd actually done something for me, and left.

Like Mississippi Vivian, he probably thought he'd thwarted me. Like her, he wasn't entirely correct. He hadn't given me any answers, but that didn't mean I couldn't look for them elsewhere, in this case John B.'s office.

I left my car parked near the post office and walked on over to John B.'s building. My bad leg wasn't bothering me too much, and I thought the walk would do it good and maybe get the rest of the soreness out of my body.

Carolyn sat at the secretary's desk, and, while she wasn't

exactly cordial, she didn't try to chase me away.

"You've been busy, Ted," she said.

I didn't have to ask what she meant. I figured tales of my exploits were all over town by now.

"This is a lively town," I said. "I don't have to look for activities to help me pass the time."

She halfway grinned. "You might have to look for friends, though."

"I consider you a friend."

"I thought I was a suspect."

She had me there. I couldn't say she wasn't. So what I said was, "Maybe not. What time does your mail carrier usually come by?"

"Around ten-thirty. Why?"

I looked at my watch. It was nearly ten-thirty already. "Mind if I stick around? I'd like to meet him."

"I guess it would be okay. John B.'s not in his office yet." This time the grin was complete. "He's a little bit under the weather today."

Because there wasn't a chair to sit on, I eased myself onto the corner of her desk. My leg was feeling all right, but it wouldn't be if I had to stand up for too long.

"I'm not surprised. A few people had a little too much to drink at the funeral home last night, and John B. might have been one of them."

"I think he might have been," Carolyn said, still grinning.

"I've been wondering about that," I said. "The drinking. Not about who had too much, but about how it got there in the first place, especially since there was a state trooper in the room."

Carolyn stopped grinning. "I'm not sure I ought to talk about that."

"It's all right," I told her. "It doesn't have anything to do with my investigation. I'm just curious."

That wasn't the absolute truth, but then a man in my profession never got anywhere if he told the absolute truth all the time.

"Well," Carolyn said, and stopped.

"Let me guess," I said. "Logan Farley has his own idea of justice and sometimes lets things slide, like Joe Bronte."

"Who said Joe let things slide?"

"I've heard it a lot," I said. Again, not absolutely true, but close enough. "It doesn't bother me. A man has his own ideas of what's right and wrong, and they don't always agree with what the law says. Nothing wrong with that."

"Not even if you're the sheriff?"

I didn't know exactly where this was going, but something in her tone made me want to keep her on the subject.

"You don't want to throw a man in jail for stealing a few sardines when he's drunk and doesn't know what he's doing."

She thought that over for a while, looking not at me but out the window at the empty street. Maybe she was looking for the mail carrier. After a while, she turned back to me and said, "What about illegal alcohol?"

"You mean he overlooks it? He wasn't even there last night."

"He knows it's being made, though. Everybody in town knows it."

I didn't, but then I hadn't been there long. I knew who she was talking about, too, and it wasn't Bronte.

"Logan Farley," I said.

"Well, yes. Like I said, everybody knows."

Farley and Bronte. I wondered just how far their willingness to ignore the law or to bend it to their own purposes went. I'd been a cop once, myself. For a long time. I'd never ignored the law, but I'd bent it a time or two, and I'd always felt bad about it. While it didn't bother me that Bronte hadn't arrested Ham Wilson for stealing sardines, I believed that the law was a kind of contract and that a lawman shouldn't break the contract. The business with the sardines was more like a loophole, no harm, no foul.

Bootlegging was a little different. In fact, it was a lot different. It wasn't something you did just to keep an impaired man from being convicted of a felony. It called for the breaking of a lot of laws, both local and federal. It was a big deal. I wondered how deeply Farley and Bronte were involved in it.

If they were, would their disregard for the law extend to cooking up an insurance scam with friends like Percy Segal and Wade Dickie? If so, it might easily enough go further, maybe leading to something like the bribery of a mail carrier, or to threatening him. I started to revise my thinking about what was going on in Losgrove.

It might be that Bronte had a lot more in mind than I'd thought when he called me to have a look at Dickie's body. Maybe he was giving me a subtle warning about how I'd end up if I didn't behave myself.

Looked at that way, everything turned upside down and the puzzle pieces scattered. I tried to look at the situation from a new perspective. Things didn't exactly fit with what I thought I'd known only minutes before, but if Bronte and Farley were running the scam, the same motives for murder would hold true, with the two lawmen as the perpetrators instead of the men I'd thought might be guilty.

Before I could get things straight in my head, the mail carrier came down the walk. He was short and compact, dressed in his summer shorts, with his worn brown leather pouch hanging from a strap slung over his shoulder. He wore granny glasses and had a face as wrinkled as a peach pit, though he couldn't have been more than forty. His short-billed cap covered most of his curly hair, but I recognized him. He'd been at the funeral home the previous night, but he was bright-eyed and chipper today. Maybe he was one of the few who hadn't been drinking. He had a magazine and a couple of letters in his hand.

He looked at me and said. "You're sitting on the mailbox."

I moved off the desk, and he laid the mail down. The magazine was some kind of legal journal. I didn't see what the letters were.

"How you doing, Ms. Lacy," he said.

He sounded almost cordial, not at all the way he'd sounded when he'd addressed me.

"I'm fine, Roy," Carolyn said, "and how about yourself?"

"Just fine. Who's your friend."

He knew how I was all right, and he didn't seem any too happy to see me.

"I'm Ted Stephens," I said. "And I can speak for myself. You can talk right to me instead of to her. You might remember me. I was at the funeral home last night."

"I remember you, all right. You caused plenty of trouble."

He didn't like me, and he didn't approve of me. Not many people did, lately.

"People keep picking on me," I said in my defense. "And me an old man."

"Not so old that you didn't lay out Johnny Turner and get poor old Wade Dickie shot again."

Carolyn snickered.

"It's not funny," Roy said. "You gotta have respect for the dead, and this fella—"

"Hold on," I said. "Johnny Turner made the first move. He's the one who swung on me, not the other way around. I didn't cause the trouble. He did."

"If you say so." Roy shook his head. "But that's not the way I saw it."

Eyewitnesses. You can't believe a word they say. Ask any trial lawyer.

"Doesn't matter to me, though," Roy continued. "I got to be on my way. 'Bye now, Ms. Lacy."

He started out of the building, and I was right behind him.

"Hold on," I said. "I'd like to talk to you."

He wasn't interested in conversation. "Got nothing to say to you. Gotta make my rounds."

"I'll just walk along with you," I told him.

"Can't let you do that. It's against the law to interfere with a federal employee in the performance of his duties."

"I'm not going to interfere. I just want to talk to you."

"Well, you can't. You try, I'm going to have to report you. If you think getting investigated by the feds is fun, you just keep talking."

"I don't want to ask you anything about your job. I just wondered if you knew a man named Percy Segal."

Roy didn't bother to turn his head to look at me. He just kept walking.

"Never heard of him."

That kind of surprised me. "I thought everybody in town knew him."

"Not me. I do my job and keep to myself. You'd best back off now. You're bothering me, and I'm not joking about calling in the postal inspectors on you."

"How about Wade Dickie? You know him?"

"I knew of him. I heard you shot him out behind the tractor place yesterday." He stopped in his tracks in front of a drugstore and pointed through the big plate-glass window. "You see that pay phone on the wall in there?"

It hung on the wall beside a shelf filled with shaving cream, razors, aftershave, and other notions.

"I see it," I said.

"Good," Roy told me. "I'm delivering the mail in there, and, if you're still bothering me when I finish, I'm getting on that phone to Mr. Stokes and turning you in."

"Well," I said, "now you've gone and scared me. I guess I'd better get myself off the streets and out of sight. Hunker down in my room until all this blows over."

He wasn't amused. "Are you trying to be funny?"

"Trying is the right word, I guess. Seems like I never quite succeed."

"Not with me you don't." He opened the drugstore door, and I felt the cool air roll outside. "I'm not going to bother delivering the mail. I'm gonna call first."

"Never mind," I said. "I was just leaving."

I left him standing there, half in and half out of the drugstore. I looked back after I'd walked a block or so, and he was still there, watching me.

I needed a place to sit and think, so I walked on down to the Magnolia Café. It wasn't time for the lunch-hour rush, so I sat in my usual spot and waited for Mississippi Vivian to come over and take my order.

"How are the Dickies?" I asked when she showed up.

"How do you think they are?" she said.

"Never mind. I have a question for you."

"I've resigned. What do you want for lunch?"

"What do you think I want?"

"Meatloaf."

"That'll do. Now about that question."

She looked around the café. No one appeared to be watching us, but that didn't seem to ease her mind.

"I shouldn't even be taking your order, much less having a conversation with you."

"Well, the truth is, I think you owe me. I don't think you earned your money."

"What do you want with that meatloaf?"

"Iced tea, green beans, mashed potatoes. And some information."

"I told you—"

I leaned forward on the table. "Never mind what you told me. It's what you didn't tell me that bothers me. You didn't tell me about the bootlegging, for one thing."

"You didn't ask me."

"I'm asking you now. Is Bronte winking at it, or is he involved in running illegal alcohol?"

"I don't know anything about that. I know moonshining goes on, but that's not the sheriff's job. That's a federal offense."

That was one way to look at it, so maybe she hadn't been holding out on me after all.

"All right," I said. "One more question. This one's about Roy the mailman."

"I know Roy. What about him?"

"He told me a few minutes ago that he didn't know Percy Segal. I thought everybody in town would have heard about his suicide."

Vivian looked at me over the tops of her glasses. "He told you he didn't know Percy?"

I should've known I'd never get two straight answers in a row from her.

"Yes, he told me he didn't know Percy. You think he does?"

"He ought to," Vivian said.

"Why's that?"

"Because Percy was his first cousin."

Chapter 24

It might seem strange to some people, but it always makes me feel good to know I've been lied to. At least when I know I'm being lied to. It lets me know I'm onto something. I wasn't sure what I was onto with the sheriff, but Roy was another story.

People lie to me for any number of reasons, but usually because they have something to hide. I figured Roy the mailman fell into that category. He didn't want to talk to me, and he was so eager to get rid of me that he threatened to call the postal inspector. Of the few things he'd told me, the main one was a lie. That didn't look good for Roy, especially as he was the one who took the mail to John B.'s office. All he had to do was deliver those letters—with their enclosed checks—to someone else. Say, Percy Segal.

Except that those checks hadn't been endorsed by Percy Segal, not even his own.

It didn't matter. I was convinced that Segal had been involved in the scam, and now I was almost convinced that Roy was in on it, too. All I had to do was figure out how. Or maybe I could just get Roy to tell me.

I paid for my meal and left the café. I didn't know Roy's route, and for all I knew he might be back at the post office by now. One thing was for sure. If he was there, nobody was going to tell me, certainly not Aubrey Stokes. Stokes wasn't going to let me look around the place, either. I could either hang around outside the building and wait to see if Roy showed up, or I could talk to Joe Bronte about my suspicions.

Or not. It was too hot to hang around, and I sure as hell didn't want to talk to Bronte. He'd either outright lied to me or misled me all along the line about a lot of things if not everything. I wasn't sure I even trusted Mississippi Vivian. So who did that leave me?

John B.? Not likely, even though I now didn't think he'd taken the letters or the checks.

Carolyn Lacy? Maybe, but she was too close to John B.

So I decided to talk to Kathy Hull. The fact that she was Carolyn's daughter bothered me a bit, but I had to take a chance on somebody, and Kathy was elected.

The tractor place wasn't busy when I entered, and I asked her if I could take her somewhere for a Coke.

"Would it be like a date?" she said.

She was teasing, but I went along with her. "You know better than that. I'm a married man. I just need to talk to somebody, and you're the only one I can think of. How about it?"

She stood up from her desk. "What do you want to talk about?"

"Johnny Turner, Roy the mailman, and a few other things."

"This has to do with your investigation?"

"It does. And it might help with figuring out who killed Wade Dickie."

"That's Joe Bronte's job."

I thought she might be joking about that, too. She'd been happy to give me the personnel files when she thought they might help find Dickie's killer.

"I know whose job it is. I'm sure Joe's out working that case right now, but I'm willing to give him a little help if I can."

"I don't guess having a Coke with you would hurt anything."

I didn't tell her that Mississippi Vivian probably wouldn't

agree. "I don't see how it could. How does Hamburger Heaven sound?"

"That would be all right, but why not the Magnolia?"

I couldn't tell her that I didn't want Mississippi Vivian to see us, so I said, "I've been hanging around there so much that I need a change."

That seemed to satisfy her. She got her purse out of the bottom desk drawer, and we left.

In Hamburger Heaven, an elderly couple sat in a back booth eating tacoburgers. I smelled the french fries and onion rings again. I wasn't sure, but I thought I could even smell jalapenos.

Aside from that one couple, no other customers were around, and that suited me just fine. I went to the counter and ordered a couple of Cokes, which came in paper cups containing more ice that soft drink, but I didn't complain. I took the cups back to where Kathy sat, set them on the table, and took a seat.

After she took a sip through the straw in her cup, Kathy said, "I'm still not quite sure what we're doing here."

"Talking," I said.

"But why me? I had the impression that you didn't much like me."

"I like you fine. I was a little worried about the way you behaved, coming to visit me in my room like you did, and then you didn't want to turn over those personnel records."

"I'm sorry about coming to your room. My father died a couple of years ago, and I got a divorce not long after that. It wasn't a friendly one. Both things were hard on my mother, and maybe I'm a little overprotective of her."

"Shouldn't that be the other way around?"

"Believe me, I don't need protecting, and I'm better off without Harry Hull. I was happy to see his taillights turn the corner. My mother thought more of him than I did. My father's death hit us both hard, but I was the one who took over and got us through it."

So she was the strong one in the family. I couldn't blame her for wanting to protect her mother from a lie-detector test. They can sometimes mislead you unless your operator is top-notch. Mine was, but Kathy had no way of knowing that.

I even understood about her not wanting to release the personnel records. They could be considered confidential, though the work records in them were the only things that interested me.

"Maybe I'm the one who overreacted," I said. "If I did, I apologize. I'd like for us to be friends because I need your help."

"If it will help you find out who killed Wade, then I'll do what I can."

We'd both finished our drinks, and I asked if she wanted another one. She didn't, and I couldn't persuade her to have an ice-cream cone, either.

"You mentioned somebody named Roy," she said. "Did you mean Roy Welling?"

I wasn't sure. "Is he a mailman?"

"Yes. He has the downtown route."

"Then that's who I meant. What can you tell me about him?"

"I don't know much about him. I see him on his route, and I know who he is, but that's all."

"He's Percy Segal's cousin, for one thing."

"I didn't know that. I don't see—" She hadn't been looking directly at me, but now her head snapped around and her eyes met mine. "I *do* see. You think that he took those letters and that he and Percy were in on some kind of deal together."

"I think Roy might have taken the letters. I'm not sure what Percy's part was."

"Then my mother's not a suspect now?"

"I've about ruled her out."

"And me?"

The older couple put their trash in a bin and left. I waited until they'd passed our table and gone through the door before I said anything.

"I think you're in the clear, too."

Kathy smiled. "I'm glad to hear it."

She must not have noticed the qualifiers I'd slipped in when I answered her questions, which was what I'd hoped. I needed her cooperation.

"Are you sure you don't know anything about Roy Welling that might help me?" I said.

"I really don't know a thing about him." She leaned back in the booth and thought it over. "I do know somebody who works at the post office, though."

That was more like it. "Who?"

"Janelle Ivie. She works at the window most of the time. I think she might have some other duties when the lobby's not busy. It's a small post office."

"So she'd know Roy."

"I'm sure she does."

She might not talk to me about him, but she'd talk to Kathy. Maybe she'd even talk to me if I was with Kathy.

"Could we drop by when she gets off work?"

Kathy had to think about that. "I guess so. She should be leaving around five."

"Good. Now about Johnny Turner."

"What about Johnny?"

"You told me once that he was under a lot of stress, but I didn't ask why. I should have. I'd like to know."

"That's kind of personal. Not to me, but to Johnny. He's the one you should talk to about it."

"Johnny doesn't like me very much."

Kathy laughed. I'm sure she'd heard an account or two of what had happened between me and Johnny at the lumberyard and later at the funeral home. Throw in our little tiff at the tractor place, and Johnny and I had an unenviable history in Losgrove, even though I'd been there only a short time.

"I'll bet you make friends wherever you go," Kathy said.

"Just about everywhere," I agreed, "but Johnny Turner isn't one of them. He's not going to talk to me. Anyway, I might already know the answer to my question, but I need you to confirm it."

"Why don't you tell me what you think, and I'll let you know if you're right."

That seemed fair enough, so I told her. "I think Johnny might have gotten Barbara Dickie pregnant. She left town either to have the baby or lose it. Now she's back, and not too happy about being here."

"You're close," Kathy said.

"How close?"

"Johnny thought the same thing you do, that Barbara was pregnant. I never believed it, though. I think Barbara would've stayed right here in town and married Johnny if that had been the case."

"Johnny might not be the marrying kind."

"Wade Dickie would've seen to it that they'd married if Barbara wanted it. Anyway, Wade and Johnny were friends, and they wouldn't have been if Johnny had gotten Barbara pregnant. Wade and Johnny worked together at the lumberyard. They even ganged up on you and beat you up."

I wondered how many different versions of that story were making the rounds. At least this one gave me credit for having fought both of them instead of just Johnny.

"You're right about the fight," I said, not bothering to correct her and explain what had really happened. "They were friends, or they seemed to be, but Wade's dead now, and, as far as I know, Johnny was the last person with him before he was killed."

"You have the wrong idea bout Johnny."

I gave her a skeptical look.

"Oh, he's a hothead, all right," she said. "Nobody who knows him would tell you anything different, but he'd never kill anybody. He's a good kid at heart."

"Maybe, and maybe he's a little soft on you to boot. That might be clouding your judgment."

"Johnny's too young for me, and he knows it. We're just sort of friendly."

"And you're sure about Barbara. She wasn't pregnant?"

"I'm as sure as I can be. I talked to her mother about it."

"When? Not today, I hope."

She shook her head. "Of course not. I went over for a while this morning, but we didn't talk about things like that, especially not with Barbara right there."

"If she wasn't pregnant," I said, "why did she leave town?"

"That's the odd thing. Ann wouldn't tell me. I asked her, but she wouldn't even talk about it."

There was something there, but I didn't know what. I'd have to think about it some more and come up with a different theory.

"Perce Segal was a well-known rounder and ladies' man," I said. "Maybe he had something to do with it."

"I wouldn't know about that. I do know he was much too old for her, though."

That was true, and I didn't think Wade would like having him hang around with her. I'd have to talk to Barbara or to Bronte to find out the rest of the story, assuming that either one of them would tell me, which was doubtful.

"One more thing," I said.

Kathy looked at her watch. "Make it quick. I have to get back to work."

"Ed Holt," I said.

"What about him?"

"He's the one who found Wade's body. Were they friends?"

"Not so much. They knew each other, like most of us in Losgrove, but I don't know that they spent much time together off the job."

"Both of them worked in Houston for a while."

"So did a lot of people."

She had me there. "You're right. Well, you've been a big help to me. I'll take you back to work."

We stood up. "I don't see how I was much of a help," she said.

"You were, though. You've helped me get some things straight in my mind, and you've given me some more things to think about. You'll be even more helpful at five o'clock when we go to the post office. While we're waiting, I'd like to have a look around the tractor place if that's okay."

"Fine by me," she said. "I just work there."

Chapter 25

I wanted to have another look around the place where Wade Dickie had been killed. I could have missed something the first time. It wasn't likely, but it was possible.

I stood under one of the big trees in the field and looked back toward the warehouse. It was cool enough in the shade of the tree, but the corrugated metal walls of the building reflected the afternoon sun into my eyes. I didn't see anything that looked like a clue. I'd been there for a good while, going over the ground, hoping that I'd get lucky, but it hadn't happened.

After a few minutes in the shade, I went around to the opposite side of the building. I didn't see anyone, but it was getting close to quitting time. Everyone had probably just about shut it down for the day and started thinking about going home.

It didn't take me long to find the restroom. It wasn't the most attractive facility of the kind I'd been inside of lately. The sink hadn't been cleaned in a while, and reddish-orange rust stains spread out around the faucets and trailed down into the bowl. The toilet wasn't any better. Though there was a cleaning brush in a small bucket of strong-smelling disinfectant sitting beside it, nobody had bothered to use it lately. Say, within the last year or so. A cheap cracked mirror hung over the sink. My reflection was distorted in the wavy glass.

The unpainted wooden floor was water-stained. I saw a tiny white chip of porcelain lying near the bucket of disinfectant and picked it up. As I turned it in my fingers, I looked around to see where it had come from. Everything looked intact, so I slipped the chip into my pocket and took the lid off the toilet tank. There was no need to be careful about fingerprints. I was sure there were fingerprints in this place that dated back to the Hoover administration.

Where the right edge of the tank lid had hung down over the top, a small flake of white was missing.

I didn't have to try fitting the piece I'd taken from the floor into the spot. I knew it would match. But, just to be sure, I set the lid on the sink and took the porcelain from my pocket. It was a match, all right, and I put it away again.

The inside of the toilet tank had never been cleaned, and slimy brown mold, or maybe it was mildew, colored the bottom and sides except in a couple of places where it had recently been rubbed away. I put the lid back on the tank and went back to the shade tree in the field.

It was still a little while until five o'clock. I sat down on the hard ground and listened to the leaves rustle above me. It was a good place to think, so that's what I did. I had a lot to think about.

Janelle Ivie was short and round, and she wore her gray hair in a bun. She looked like somebody's grandmother, and she probably was. I could picture her in a flour-spotted apron, baking bread.

Kathy and I met her as she was leaving work, and Kathy explained who I was and what I was doing there.

Janelle looked me up and down. "You don't look much like somebody who'd let Johnny Turner beat him up."

"It didn't happen quite that way," I told her. I didn't sigh, but I felt like it. "I'll trade you the real story for a little conversation."

"About what?"

"About Roy Welling."

She made a disapproving noise.

"You don't like him?" I said.

"Never you mind who I like. If I can help you with your investigation, I will."

"We need a place to talk," I said.

"My house," she said. "Just follow me."

She got into a black '69 Chevy Camaro and peeled out of the parking lot. Maybe I'd misjudged her.

"I'm too slow to follow her," I said.

Kathy laughed. "That's all right. I know where she lives."

As it turned out, she lived not too far from the Dickies, in a house with a wide front porch with a swing hanging from the ceiling on silvery chains. A couple of green metal chairs were close by. Janelle was already sitting in the swing by the time we got there. Kathy and I sat in the chairs.

"What do you want to know about Roy?" Janelle said when we were seated.

I explained more about what I was doing in town, with the emphasis on the missing letters.

Janelle pushed her right foot on the porch and put the swing in gentle motion. The chains creaked a bit in the hooks that held them.

"Roy'd be in big trouble if he was messing with the mail," she said. "Postal inspectors don't like that kind of thing. Roy might land in jail."

"I expect he will," I said. "If he's been doing anything wrong, that is. You think he would?"

"Would he what?"

"Do anything wrong."

"Anybody will do something wrong if he thinks he can make money from it. Roy's no different." She made the disapproving noise again. "More likely than some, I expect."

I needed more than her disapproval, however. I needed something I could investigate or something I could take to the law. Janelle said she didn't have anything like that for me, but she didn't think it mattered.

"You don't need anything else. The postal inspectors will take care of it for you if he's been taking letters. They'll come down on him like a ton of bricks."

"I know that, but the company I represent wouldn't want to wait for them to get it done. I was in the Army, and I know how the government is. It could be five years before they complete an investigation."

"I wish I could help," Janelle said, sounding genuinely sorry, "but I don't know what I can do. All Roy had to do was pocket those letters while he walked his route. It would've been easy to do. I'm sure nobody at the PO ever saw him take them. They'd have reported him if they had."

I was getting frustrated, but I tried not to show it. "What about his friends? Aside from Percy Segal, that is."

"He was good friends with Wade Dickie. Those two were real close. I'm sure Wade's killing has him pretty shaken up."

That was something, I supposed. Segal, Dickie, and Welling. I was sure they'd all been in on the scheme.

"How about Ed Holt?" I said. "Did Roy know him?"

"Oh, sure. Roy and Perce and Ed and Wade had a poker group. They played at least a couple of times a month. Roy mentioned it now and then. When he won, mostly. He didn't talk about losing."

"Just good old boys together," I said.

"That's right. They're all good old boys." She realized what she'd said. "Well, they *were* all good old boys. Two of them are gone now."

"Seems a little suspicious, doesn't it," I said.

She put her foot down on the porch and stopped the swing.

"Stuff happens." She stood up. "I have to fix supper now. I won't say anything to Roy about our talk."

Kathy and I stood up, too. I said, "I appreciate that. I wish I had a picture of that sucker."

"What for?"

"To show around at some places where I think he cashed checks."

"I have a picture."

I hadn't expected that. "You do?"

"We both got a service award a couple of years ago. Got our picture in the paper and everything. I have the picture."

"I'd sure like to see it."

"You just wait here," she said.

She went into the house, leaving me and Kathy on the porch.

"Do you think the picture will help?"

"If I can get anyone to identify him, at the places where he cashed those checks, my case is solved. Even if it's out of Bronte's hands and mine, my boss will be satisfied. He can stop sending the checks, and that's all he cares about."

Janelle came back out, holding a framed black-and-white photo. She handed it to me and said, "That's Roy on the right."

I grinned. Her jokes were almost as bad as mine. "Can I borrow this?"

"Long as you don't lose it. I'm proud of getting that award."

"I'll bring it back to you tomorrow," I promised, and she said I could take it with me.

Kathy and I left. We were in my rental, so I dropped her off at the tractor place before heading for the drugstore. The banks were closed, and I wasn't sure where the other places were, but the drugstore was right on the main street. One of the checks had been cashed there every month.

I might need the picture at other places, but not there. Welling delivered their mail, and everyone would know him. That would have made it easy for him to cash a two-party check there.

The clerk at the cash register was willing to talk to me after I identified myself and told him what I was in town for. Like nearly everybody else, he'd heard about me.

"You're the one who got his tail kicked over at the lumberyard," he said with a grin.

"Right. You Losgrove boys are too tough for us big-city fellas."

He looked me over carefully. "I can see why it took two of 'em. I don't think I'd like to take you on by myself."

I told him I appreciated the thought and asked if Roy Welling had ever cashed a two-party check there.

He didn't even have to think it over. "I can tell you right now that Roy never cashed an insurance check in here."

I should've known it wouldn't be that easy. Roy was too well known around town. Hell, he delivered mail to the drugstore. He'd know better than to cash one of the insurance checks there.

"I remember those checks, though," the cashier said.

I perked up a little. Maybe my luck was changing.

"Fella came in with one of them every month," the cashier went on. "Reason I noticed, the check was always made out to Dub Darrow, but that wasn't who cashed it."

Darrow's name was on my list of claimants. Things were indeed looking up.

"The fella that cashed the check said he worked for Dub," the cashier continued, "and Dub always paid him with the insurance checks. Ann Dickie vouched for the fella, said Wade knew him and it was all on the up-and-up."

That just about cinched things for me. Ann Dickie was in on the scam, or, if she wasn't, Wade had told her to vouch for the man who cashed the checks.

"You remember the name of the man who had Darrow's

checks?" I asked.

"I hope I'm not going to get in any trouble about this," he said.

I told him he wasn't and asked about the man who'd cashed the checks.

"His name's Doug Crombie. Doesn't live around here, far as I know. Might've come in from out of town to do that work for Dub. The fella you're asking about, Roy Welling, he knew him, though."

"He did? Are you sure about that?"

"Pretty sure. This Crombie always seemed to come in right after Roy brought the mail by. I never thought anything about it until right this minute. I'll tell you something else. One day I went outside right after I cashed his check, and he and Roy were standing right next door, talking and laughing like they were old buddies."

That clinched it for me. It might not be enough for the postal inspectors or Joe Bronte, but I was sure I'd found out what was going on. Percy Segal, Wade Dickie, and Ed Holt were in on things together. Maybe Ann Dickie, too.

It was probably Percy's scheme to begin with. He got the men to come to work in Houston, and it would have been easy enough for him or someone else to make the job unattractive enough for them to quit. Then Percy would file the claims himself.

He'd brought the others in on it because it had been too big an operation. I still wasn't sure of the precise details, but I'd have bet my pay from National that was how it worked. Roy took the letters, got somebody to cash the checks, and they all split the proceeds. I doubted if any of the other men who'd supposedly filed claims even knew the checks had been sent.

I didn't have enough on Holt. In fact, I had nothing other than suspicion, but my suspicion had been firming up for a good while. Sometimes it's the little things that trip you up, and in Holt's case it was the faint red line on his face when I saw him at the funeral home. I was pretty sure it had been made by the seam of a stocking pulled over his head as a disguise. I figured him for one of the men in the pickup that ran me off the road. Welling might have been the other.

I thanked the cashier for his help and left the drugstore. I had to decide what to do next. Maybe Don Cogsdill could help me make up my mind. I decided to skip dinner. I went back to the motel to give Don a call.

"You don't trust the sheriff?" Don said. "Why not?"

"Just take my word for it," I said. "It's too complicated to explain on the phone."

"All right. So you don't trust him. What do you have in mind."

I told him.

"It's risky," he said. "Might not work. Might get your ass thrown in jail."

"I won't push it that far," I said, hoping I was telling the truth. I was going to get Welling to talk, one way or the other.

"All right, then, but be careful. And no breaking and entering."

"I promise," I said, not really meaning it. I was tired of being jacked around by half the population of Losgrove, Mississippi. I'd do whatever it took, and if that meant breaking into Welling's house, I was up for it.

"You know the company can't be responsible for you," Don said. "We'll provide bail money, of course, if they toss you in the clink. We might even hire you a lawyer. But that's it. We're not taking responsibility for what you do from this point on."

I wasn't surprised. In fact, I'd expected him to say something like that. I didn't mind. It was all part of the job.

"I want you to write out a document that says you're acting

on your own," Don said. "Be sure to sign it. You might even get it notarized. That would be a nice touch."

"I don't know any notaries here, much less one that would do the job this late. You'll just have to trust me to do it and hope it'll hold up in court if things go that far."

"You know I trust you, Ted." He tried to sound apologetic, but he didn't quite manage it. "I'm just trying to cover my ass."

The last part was sincere. I didn't blame him for that, either. I told Don that and said, "I'll write something out. It'll make it clear that I'm acting on my own. Hell, I'll even say you told me not to do whatever it is that I'm going to do."

"I'm sure it'll be airtight. Let me know what happens."

"You'll be among the first to hear," I said.

Chapter 26

After I hung up, I called Sarah and told her that things were going fine, just fine.

"Does that mean you'll be home soon?" she asked.

"I'll be wrapping things up any day now," I said.

I didn't feel it was necessary to mention that I might wind up in jail. No need to worry her. I told her that I loved her and that I'd see her in a day or so. After all, if I was in jail, surely she'd pay me a visit.

The next item on my agenda was a visit to Roy Welling. I looked him up in the phone book and discovered that he lived in town. I didn't have any trouble finding the place. It was on the opposite side of town from the Dickies and Janelle Ivie, but the house was from the same era. I hadn't seen any really new houses since I'd been in town.

Welling's house was well kept up. Fresh paint, landscaped yard, new roof. I wasn't surprised. He had plenty of money to spend on it. A two-car garage was attached to the side of the house, both doors pulled down. I wondered what kind of cars he owned.

I parked the Plymouth at the curb and got out. The humid air was heavier than usual, and dark clouds massed in the sky to the north. A sliver of lightning flickered through the clouds, followed by the distant rumble of thunder.

I went right up to Welling's front door and rang the bell, just like I was a good friend that he was expecting to pay him a visit.

The look on his face when he opened the door and saw me, however, wasn't one with which he'd have greeted a friend of any kind.

"I'm calling the cops," he said.

"That's no way to welcome a visitor," I said.

I put my hand on his chest and gave a gentle push. He stepped back into his house, and I followed him right in. We were in a narrow entry hall floored with dark-green tile. To my left was a small living room. The den was in front of us. Welling turned and went into the living room.

I went with him. The shag carpet was brand new. I could smell the carpet glue. Bookcases lined one wall, but there were no books in them. They held only a few knickknacks: round glass paperweights filled with ribbons of color; some framed photographs, including the same one Janelle Ivie had given me; a few ceramic figures of horses, and one of a duck. Why a duck? I wondered.

Welling didn't look at the bookcases. He headed for the telephone on a little stand at one end of a beige couch. He picked up the phone and said, "I'll give you ten seconds. Then I'm calling Joe Bronte."

I sat in an uncomfortable armchair. "Go right ahead and make that call. I'd like to talk to him, too."

That wasn't what Welling wanted to hear. "You think I'm joking? You're interfering with a federal employee. Bronte will arrest you."

"No, he won't. You're at home, and you're off the job. Besides, Bronte doesn't enforce the federal laws. I'm not sure just which ones he does enforce, but not those."

I leaned back and crossed my legs. The chair was turning out to be more comfortable than I'd thought, after all.

"Here's what I know," I said. I'd decided on the direct approach. "I know that every month you steal the insurance checks addressed to people in care of John B. Campbell's office and get someone else to cash them. Doug Crombie's the someone else."

Welling put the phone back in its cradle.

"That's better," I said. "Why don't you have a sit-down so we can talk."

It must have sounded as if we were in my house instead of his. He sat on the edge of the couch, his clasped hands hanging between his slightly spread legs. He looked at me expectantly.

"I know that Percy Segal was behind things to begin with," I said. "Dickie and Holt were in on it, too. I don't know if you were part of it from the beginning or not, but it doesn't matter. You're in on it now."

A clap of thunder rattled the windows. The rain was getting closer. It was late afternoon, and the room was getting dark.

Welling ignored the thunder. I thought he might turn on a light, but he also ignored the gathering darkness.

"I don't know what you're talking about," he said.

I had to laugh. Give the guy credit for trying to brazen it out.

"Sure you do," I said. "It'll be easy to prove." I hoped I sounded more confident of that than I actually was. "I'm turning everything I have in to your postmaster, and he can pass it along to the postal inspectors."

"It won't do you any good."

"Maybe not. We'll have to see." I paused to let him think it over. Then I said, "Here's something else I know."

I didn't know everything, of course, but I figured it would be pretty close to the truth. If I was right, maybe he'd tell me. If I wasn't, maybe he'd give me a hint. Or maybe he'd just laugh at me.

"You deliver the mail to John B. Campbell's office every day," I said.

"Big deal. It's on my route. So what?"

"So you have easy access to the secretary's desk. A lot of the time when you come in, she's not there. I think you took some letterhead stationery from it one day when she was gone. Nobody would ever miss eight or ten sheets of it. I think you or someone else wrote the claim letters on that letterhead and sent them to National Insurance in Houston. Most of the people who were supposedly hurt on the job didn't even know you'd used their names. All I have to do is ask them."

"They'd just lie to you."

Another clap of thunder sounded, and rain began to pelt the roof of the house.

"They might lie to me, sure," I said, "but I could find out easily enough if they'd ever received those checks or if Doug Crombie had cashed them. All I have to do is ask around."

Welling sighed as if he was getting tired of listening to me.

"It's time for you to leave now," he said.

"Not quite. I'd like to know if Mrs. Dickie was in on things. She's the one who vouched for Crombie at the drugstore."

The rain fell in sheets that washed down from the roof and rushed past the living-room window.

"You can go to hell," Welling said.

The rain hadn't improved his mood. I guessed he wasn't going to tell me about Ann Dickie, but I still had a few questions even if it didn't do me any good to ask them.

"I'd also like to know who killed Percy Segal and Wade Dickie," I said. "Was it a case of thieves falling out, or was it something else?"

The house was cool, but Welling started to sweat.

"I don't have any idea about that," he said.

"Okay, let's say you're telling the truth, not that I think you are. You don't happen to own a beat-up old pickup, do you? It'd be a little more beat up today than it was last night, seeing as how you tried to kill me with it."

Sweat beaded his forehead, but he didn't move to do anything about it.

"I don't have any pickup," he said.

"Be easy enough for me to find out. Just a quick trip to the courthouse. Even easier than that, I could look in your garage."

He jumped me then. I should've been ready for it, but I wasn't. He launched himself across the coffee table and knocked me over before I could move. The chair and I tumbled over backward with Welling on top.

He wasn't big, but he was wiry. He wrapped his legs around my body while I was tangled in the chair. He clamped his hands on my throat and started to squeeze. He had a powerful grip, maybe from hauling that leather mailbag.

I don't really have any excuse for his getting the better of me like that, but I'd had a rough night, and I still hadn't recovered. Okay, that's an excuse, but it's the truth.

I hammered the side of his head a couple of times with the heel of my hand while he strangled me, but it didn't bother him a bit as far as I could tell. My throat was constricted, and I couldn't take in enough air for even a wheeze. I had to do something fast or I wouldn't be there anymore.

I hit him again. This time I got a little rougher. I tried to drive the knuckle of my index finger through his temple.

That shook him for a second, and his grip loosened. I sucked in air and hit him again. He rolled off me, and I escaped the overturned chair.

Welling jumped to his feet. He was a spry little rascal.

I wasn't spry at all. I stayed on the floor and grabbed for his ankle. I missed and he jerked his foot out of the way. He snatched a paperweight from the bookshelf and threw it at me. It was heavy and hard, and it hit my shoulder like a bullet. If it had hit me in the head, it would have put me out and it might even have put me under. I rolled over a couple of times and tried to get behind the chair.

Welling threw another paperweight, but it bounced off the chair. The room was dark, and the rain fell in torrents outside. Welling was little more than a dark shape on the other side of the room, but I could tell that he was reaching for another paperweight. If this kind of thing kept happening, I was going to have to reconsider my not carrying a sidearm.

On the other hand, if this kind of thing kept up, I might not be around to reconsider anything. I had to do something about Welling before he brained me with a hunk of glass, so I braced both legs against the chair and shoved it at him.

It slid over the rug more smoothly than I'd thought it would and hit Welling in the shins. He lost his balance and fell across it, dropping the paperweight, which bounced once and rolled across the carpet toward me.

I stuck out a hand and made a grab at the paperweight. I touched it, but I couldn't hold it. The smooth glass slipped away from me into the hall and bonked across the tiled floor.

Welling jumped to his feet and then jumped over the chair. His next move would be to jump back on top of me, so I slithered off after the paperweight. My fingers touched it, and I got a good grip on it. I rolled over and threw it at Welling without even looking.

It hit him right in the middle of the forehead with a satisfying *thunk* like the sound of a hammer hitting wood. If I'd been trying, I could never have scored a hit like that, but I wasn't going to tell anyone.

I wouldn't have to tell Welling because he couldn't have heard me if I'd tried. He fell straight forward and landed on his face with his head about six inches from me. Something crunched, probably his nose. I didn't feel bad about that at all.

Welling lay still, and so I grabbed hold of the door frame and hauled myself into a seated position and took stock. I didn't seem to be in any worse shape than I'd been when I'd come into the house, except for my throat, which hurt when I swallowed.

I stood up. Since I didn't fall down, I figured everything was working as it should be. I looked around for a light switch. I located it on the wall to my right and flipped it. When the light came on, I knelt down and rolled Welling over on his back. His nose looked flattened, all right, but it wasn't bleeding. I wouldn't have cared if it was. Since he seemed to be sleeping peacefully, I left him lying there. I turned on the overhead light and went to sit on his couch to think things over. I had to decide whether to make a call to Joe Bronte.

I could always just leave Welling where he was, present my case to the postmaster, and let the postal inspectors take over. There were a lot of things wrong with that idea. The inspectors might be slow to move, and, by the time they even started an investigation, Welling would be somewhere else, Mexico, maybe, or Canada.

I was convinced I'd solved the mystery of the checks, and I knew Don Cogsdill would see it that way, too. National Insurance would make no more payments on the false claims. I didn't think they'd have much luck recovering any of the money they'd already paid out, but I knew they'd try. That wasn't my problem, and I didn't worry about it.

One thing that did worry me was Bronte, and, to a lesser extent, Farley. Were they involved in the scam? And if they were, how deep did their involvement run?

The fact that they knew about the bootlegging and allowed it to go on didn't mean much by itself. They might have believed that a little corn liquor never hurt anybody. Plenty of people in the South still thought that way, and bootleggers were heroes to some of them.

Even if Farley and Bronte didn't think that way, they might

have thought it was the job of the feds to shut down any stills in the area. If that was the case, okay, I could understand it. But why did Bronte lie to me about Mrs. Dickie when she came to see her husband's body? And what about the other times he'd lied or tried his hardest to steer me away from the truth?

I thought I had the answer now, but I wasn't certain. Maybe Bronte would tell me if I confronted him with it.

The fact was that I needed the law. I had Welling, and I could file charges on him for assault, if nothing else, and get him locked up until the feds could deal with him.

As if he'd heard my thoughts, Welling snored and rolled onto his side. A big knot had risen on his forehead where the paperweight had struck him. It would be very colorful in a few hours. I watched him for a second, but he didn't wake up.

Besides Welling, there was Holt, who in all likelihood had killed Wade Dickie. Holt had gone to the restroom that afternoon, just as he'd said, but he hadn't gone to answer nature's call. I was certain he'd gone to pick up the pistol he'd hidden in the toilet tank earlier. He'd called Dickie to meet him behind the warehouse, and, when Dickie got there, Holt shot him. Then he took the pistol back to the restroom and hid it again, wrapped up in plastic, no doubt.

I could think of several reasons why Holt might have killed Dickie, but I suspected that mainly it was because Dickie was getting worried about me and what I was uncovering. He'd probably been worried from the beginning, especially considering what I might find out about Segal's death.

When I'd visited with Dickie and Turner, just before our little tussle, I'd told him that I wanted to talk to him about Percy Segal. He must have known then that I was onto them and that eventually I'd figure things out. It wasn't all that complicated.

He must have mentioned his misgivings to Holt more than

once, and that was all it took. Holt had gotten him out of the way.

Holt had also tried to get rid of me, but that hadn't worked out.

Dickie should have talked to me about the death of Percy Segal. I'd developed what I believed was a solid theory about that death, and while I had a feeling Dickie would have wanted me out of town before I made sure I was right, he needn't have worried about that. I wouldn't have done anything. I'd have left that up to the ones involved, including Bronte. I wasn't there to clean up the town. I just wanted to do my job.

To do that, I was going to have to trust someone besides Kathy Hull.

I picked up the phone and called the sheriff's office.

CHAPTER 27

It had stopped raining by the time Bronte arrived at Welling's house. He and Deputy Ellis stood in the doorway looking at Welling, who sat on the couch with his head in his hands and said not a word. The minions of the law didn't have anything to say, either.

I sat in the armchair, which I'd set back upright. I was just as quiet as everyone else. I didn't want to be the first.

Bronte and Ellis had come in together, and neither of them looked particularly happy to be there. When they saw Welling, they looked even less happy.

Bronte turned to me. "Well?" he said.

"Well," I said, glad that someone had broken the silence, "I confronted him with the evidence that he was a big part of the insurance scam I've been investigating. He has a bad temper, I think. Anyway, he jumped me and threw a couple of paperweights at me. I threw one back at him. That's about it."

"This evidence you told him about. Do you have it with you?"

"Not exactly," I said, and I went through my reasoning with him. "All you have to do is ask at the places where Crombie cashed the checks. That'll give you Crombie, and when you pick him up he'll give you what you need on Welling. You might look around in here and see if Welling kept any of John B.'s stationery for emergencies. That'll give you some more evidence."

"Not much. Anybody could have something like that."

"Along with everything else, it'll help convince a jury. For now, though, you can just hold him on the assault charges I'll be filing."

I didn't really care whether Bronte filed charges on Welling for the scam or not. Frank Briscoe and Carol Vance would take care of that back in Houston if need be. I already had Frank's word on that.

"Are you saying that Welling was the ringleader of that insurance scam?" Bronte said.

"No. I think that was someone else, one of three people. Or they could all have been equal partners. Wade Dickie, Percy Segal, and Ed Holt. Holt's the one who killed Dickie, by the way. Just in case you haven't figured that out yet."

Bronte was a bit surprised by that last bit of news. "Just how in the hell do you know that?"

I explained my reasoning and said, "If you get a search warrant tonight, I think you can find the pistol that killed Dickie. It'll be at Holt's house. He wouldn't have ditched it. Not yet. If he hears about Welling, though, you can bet that he will."

"What do you think, Ellis?" Bronte said.

Ellis, who'd kept quiet up to that point, said, "I think he might be right."

"Pretty flimsy evidence. You think you can get a warrant?"

"Judge Harken will go for it," Ellis said.

"Take care of it, then. Take plenty of backup. Arrest Holt if you find the gun."

"If it's there," Ellis said, "I'll find it."

I didn't doubt it, and I'm sure Bronte didn't, either.

Bronte motioned toward Welling and said to Ellis, "You might as well take Roy by the jail first and book him into a cell."

Ellis nodded. He went over to the couch and helped Welling to his feet, then cuffed his hands behind him. Welling didn't show any resistance. He didn't have any fight left in him. A good solid blow to the head will do that to a man.

"That's quite a knot on his head," Bronte said.

"You might want to get him looked at by a doctor," I said. "He could have a concussion."

"His nose doesn't look so good, either," Ellis said.

"The doctor could look at it. I think it's broken."

"We'll get him booked first, have a doctor come in later," Bronte said. "We need to get to Holt before he gets word of this."

Ellis led Welling out of the room. Welling's step wasn't as spry as it had been.

"I guess that wraps things up for you, Stephens," Bronte said after Ellis and Welling were gone. "You've got your perps all taken care of. Two of them are dead, we have one in custody, and we'll have the third one locked up before the night's over if we find that gun. Now you can go on home to Houston."

He sounded happy about the prospect of my leaving his little town. For some reason people always seemed to be glad to see me go. I like to think they miss me when I'm gone, though.

"Not everything is taken care of," I said. I hated to take away his pleasure, but I wasn't ready to leave town. Not quite. "I don't like loose ends, and there's one thing still dangling."

Bronte cocked his head. "And that would be?"

"Percy Segal."

"He's dead. Even if he was part of this mess, it's too late to arrest him now."

"I know that. I also know who killed him."

It was more a likelihood than certain knowledge, but, the way things stacked up, I was morally certain I had the answer, and it explained a lot of things that had been bothering me. Sometimes if you wait for the absolute truth to show itself, the train's already left the station.

"Perce shot himself," Bronte said, looking away from me.

"No," I said. "We both know better than that. He was shot, all right, but by someone else. Barbara Dickie."

Her behavior that morning had been my final hint. A man doesn't go to another man's house and kill himself. That had been ridiculous from the start. People believed it, if they did, because they wanted to.

"It was a self-inflicted wound," Bronte said, still looking away.

"That's what you called it. At first I thought Dickie might have killed him. A thieves-fall-out deal, but it wasn't that. Percy was a womanizer, and he went over to Dickie's place for some reason and found Barbara home alone. Maybe that's why he went, because he knew she was there by herself. He tried something. Must have carried it way too far, and she killed him. You covered it up. How many people know?"

"That's not the way it happened. He shot himself."

"You can keep saying it, and I'll keep not believing it. I saw how Barbara reacted today. She hated Percy even worse than other people I've talked to, and they didn't like him even a little bit. I figure her mother knows, and Wade knew. That might be all, unless Farley's in on it."

"Farley? What's he got to do with anything?"

"You and he are the main law around here. You run things your way. If you see something you think's wrong, you bend the law a little. Bootlegging would be one example."

"If you're talking about the drinking at the funeral home, that's more or less the custom here. It doesn't hurt anything."

I thought about Farley pulling his gun and shooting Dickie's body.

"Good thing Dickie wasn't alive, or he'd be dead again."

"You don't approve of me and Farley," Bronte said.

"It's not my business to approve or disapprove. I don't vote here. It seems to me, though, that you're sworn to uphold the law, and you don't always do it. I'm not sure that's right."

"You were a cop once. You know how it is."

I'd been a cop, and I'd bent the law a time or two, all right. Not when it came to murder, though.

"You go on back to Houston," Bronte said. "Even if you're right about Segal, and I'm not saying you are, it's way too late for you to do anything about it."

He had me there. I could go to the newspaper, but they probably wouldn't even print the story. The editor might believe Bronte had done the right thing.

"You could have turned it over to a grand jury," I said. "They'd never have indicted her, and it would've been cleaner."

"You don't know everything, Stephens, even if you think you do. Barbara had a reputation. Everybody on the grand jury would have known it. Some of them would have believed she led Segal on. Maybe all of them. It would've been messy."

"If it had happened," I said.

"Right. Which it didn't."

"Maybe she did lead him on."

"Maybe this, maybe that. Doesn't matter. It's over. Go home, Stephens."

I thought about it for a while. Bronte didn't have anything else to say, so I left.

I got a call from Ellis early the next morning. I didn't have to wonder why Bronte himself didn't call. He had nothing more to say to me.

"I found the gun," Ellis said. "We'll have to do a ballistics check, but I think Holt's good for the killing. He might even decide to confess."

"While you have out the rubber hose," I said, "be sure to ask him about filing those false claims."

"Won't have to. Roy Welling's already told us all about it. We arrested Crombie last night, too. It didn't take ten minutes in a cell for him to crack. He's pretty much confirmed your suspicions about the insurance deal."

"Sounds like my work here is done," I said.

"And not a minute too soon," Ellis said. "I don't think Joe likes you very much."

"He won't be sheriff forever."

"He is, now, though. See you around, Stephens."

I didn't think so. I wasn't planning on coming back to Losgrove, though I might have to if there were any little things about the case that needed to be cleared up later.

"Maybe," I said.

Before I left town, I went back to the Magnolia Café for breakfast.

"What's good today?" I asked when Mississippi Vivian came to my table.

"What do you think?" she said, which was pretty much what I'd expected.

"Biscuits and gravy, sausage, and coffee," I said.

"Anything else?"

"What do you think?"

She grinned and looked at me over the tops of her glasses. "We're going to miss you around here, Ted."

So the word was already out. I should have known. I wondered just how much she knew, or suspected, about Barbara Dickie and Percy Segal's death. I knew one thing for sure: Whatever it was, she'd never tell me.

"Are you going to miss me, or my money?" I said.

I didn't intend it as an insult, and she didn't take it as one.

"I'll miss you both. I'm sorry I wasn't as good an informant as you expected, but I didn't want to get myself in trouble."

"Now how could you have done that?"

"There might not be any secrets in Losgrove," Mississippi

Vivian said. "But there are things we don't talk about."

She left me to turn in the order, and, after a few minutes, when she brought it to the table, she had nothing else to say. I ate and listened to the hum of the talk of the other customers, none of whom looked my way. The food was good, as usual. I was going to miss the Magnolia Café.

As I was draining my coffee cup, Mississippi Vivian came over and said, "Don't worry about the check, Ted. It's my treat. It's been nice knowing you."

I stood up and thanked her for the breakfast. As I walked out the door, she called, "Y'all come back, you hear?"

I turned and gave her a Boy Scout salute.

"Maybe," I said.

ABOUT THE AUTHORS

Bill Crider is the multiple Anthony Award–winning author of the Sheriff Dan Rhodes series. He has published more than fifty mystery, Western, and horror novels under his own and other names.

Clyde Wilson was a former Houston, Texas, private eye, a legendary figure whose cases involved the famous and the infamous. He passed away on November 1, 2008.